REIGNITED

BY COLLEEN HOUCK

ALSO BY COLLEEN HOUCK

TIGER'S SAGA

Tiger's Promise

Tiger's Curse

Tiger's Quest

Tiger's Voyage

Tiger's Destiny

REAWAKENED SERIES

Reawakened

Recreated

Reignited

Reunited

REIGNITED

Published by Colleen Houck

Love's Pretense

An Ancient Egyptian
Love Poem

With sickness faint
and weary
All day in bed I'll lie;
My friends will gather
near me
And she'll with them
come nigh.

She'll put to shame the
doctors
Who'll ponder over
me,
For she alone, my
loved one,
Knows well my
malady.

***From Egyptian Myths And Legend**

By Donald Mackenzie

The Dove Song

An Ancient Egyptian
Love Poem

I hear thy voice, O
turtle dove-
The dawn is all aglow-
Weary am I with love,
with love,
Oh, whither shall I go?

Not so, O beauteous
bird above,
Is joy to be denied....
For I have found my
dear, my love;
And I am by his side.

We wander forth, and
hand in hand
Through flowery ways
we go-
I am the fairest in the
land,
For he has called me
so.

Dedication

For Becca, Sam, and Josh

Who taught me to love *Doctors*

PROLOGUE

RIPENING

Seth crouched down to peer at the face of the mortal woman trembling at his feet. It had been an accident—a wonderful, terrible, incredible accident. Euphoria and horror twisted together inside him, until he was almost physically sick from the emotional turmoil of what he'd done. From what he…was.

Centuries had passed with no sign that Seth was ever going to come into his powers. Osiris – tall and handsome with his chiseled jaw and quick smile, everyone's favorite hero – had been flaunting his abilities since he was a strapping boy. Isis – Seth's beautiful, glorious, and chilling sister – was every inch the untouchable and perfect goddess.

If he'd had even a fraction of her ability to cast spells and manipulate magic, he'd thank the stars and be happy with his lot.

Even Nephthys, as unassuming as her gifts were, had developed a talent as a seer and an ability to discern the messages of the stars long before he had come into his own.

It wasn't fair.

Seth stood and clenched his fists as he thought of it, ignoring the writhing woman prostrating herself before him.

He was the last born. The youngest. It wasn't his fault that the Waters of Chaos had been nearly emptied by the time he was born, and yet he was the one who had paid the price. While his siblings learned to hone their burgeoning skills and spent their evenings showing off to one another, all he could do was watch them enviously, chest tight and jaw clenched, wondering when, or even if, he would ever find his place in the universe.

During his awkward adolescence – which lasted aeons longer for gods than for mortals, since the spans of their lives were more consistent with those of stars – he'd practice fixedly for days and weeks at a time, never taking sustenance or resting until he'd crumple with exhaustion and fall into the valley of his father's chest looking for respite. He'd hoped that his father would at least acknowledge his efforts, perhaps take note of the prickly sweat that ran down the back of his neck and his overheated red face. But the god of the earth cared not for such things and, in fact, viewed his youngest son's painful lack of progress as less than godlike.

When Seth complained and begged audience, his father, Geb, answered with merely a rumble of the ground, if he bothered to answer at all. Gradually, Seth stopped seeking out his guiding hand.

He next turned his eyes to the sky and cried out to his mother who looked down upon him, the clouds of her hair stirring. There was nothing she could do to comfort him except offer her tears. Salty drops would fall and soon he'd be sitting in a pool of her sorrow. No. Geb and Nut would not help him.

Once, he'd turned to his grandfather for advice. But Shu, the god of the wind, just told him to quit his whining and get on with being the god he was. If he couldn't manage that, then he should try to act more like his older brother, Osiris. And to top off his remarks, Shu sent a stiff gale to dry young Seth's tears but the hot wind buffeted him, driving him halfway across the Earth before he managed to muster enough strength to resist the powerful push of his elder.

It wasn't long before he stopped seeking their aid altogether. Over time Seth withdrew from associating with his elders and his siblings and ignored their summons to participate in the drawn-out meetings of the newly organized Ennead.

What did he care for the plight of mortals or of the governing of the cosmos? What had the cosmos ever done for him? Besides, he couldn't stand to see the pitying looks from his sisters, or, worse, see their giddy expressions of delight whenever Osiris graced the halls of Heliopolis with his presence.

In fact, the only reason he'd visited Heliopolis at all in the last century was to watch Isis. Seth had spent many long nights reclining in the leafy branches of the tree that brushed against her window. Often, she was away, attending to one duty or another that the ruler of all the gods, Amun-Ra, assigned her. He'd leave the tree disappointed, with an uncomfortable crick in his neck that a god of any reputation shouldn't be at all bothered by. But, every once in a while, his patience was rewarded and he would get an unobstructed view of the ice princess as she prepared to retire for the evening.

At first, he'd spied on her to try to learn her secrets, memorize the spells she'd create and practice before bed. But he soon found that no matter how meticulous he was, or how precise he'd been in copying the spell, he just could not wield magic the same way she did. Even so, he was still drawn to her and found himself outside her window more often than not.

Isis was cold, lovely, and formidable. Seth considered her the most gifted of the siblings. As he sat uncomfortably, night after night, he imagined that he could snatch away her abilities and take them into himself. He would twist her magic and use it to suit his own purposes. Then no one would look at him with sympathy or wince at seeing his bumbling attempts with manipulating matter. Not if he had the gifts of Isis at his disposal.

In the beginning, Seth envisioned taking her power. Then, as time went on and he grew into manhood, his fantasies twisted. He fed his admittedly unwholesome and unnatural obsession with Isis to the point of ignoring his own physical needs. Starving was painful but it wouldn't kill him and the others either didn't care about or didn't notice the dark smudges beneath his eyes and the lankness of his hair. And no one paid him any attention at all whenever Osiris was around anyway.

As he perched in the shadows of his tree, watching her brush her hair, he'd summon a tiny wind – something so unnoticeable as to be considered a non-talent and yet it still took a great deal of his energy – to lift the perfume from her delicate neck. It raced toward his hand where he'd capture it, holding it close to his face until it dissipated hours later.

Then, giving in to the object he kept hidden during the day, Seth would pull out the feather he'd taken from her bath and stroke it, his thumb running over the soft plume in a slow loop as he thought of the one it belonged to. When Isis finally slept, he'd make himself as comfortable as he could and keep silent vigil, allowing his secret, dark thoughts to take shape and embed their vacillating roots in his mind.

If he'd been more confident, he would have done something about his feelings years ago. He would have confronted Isis. Shown her that Osiris was not worth the attention she gave him. That true desire was much more than a winning smile and broad shoulders.

No.

True desire was the trembling he felt in his limbs when he looked at her, the need to absorb her completely into himself. To fashion a world where only the two of them existed, one where they could step into their proper places as king and queen of the cosmos and have all others kneel at their feet and worship them. That's what he envisioned when he looked at Isis. There was no one else worthy of him.

Especially now that he had finally come into his own power. Despite all the exhaustion, anxiety, and fear that had crippled him because it had taken so long to appear, Seth realized that it had all been worth it. For his ability was the most terrible and fantastic of all – he had the power to unmake.

It was evidenced in the form of the writhing woman on the ground. Seth had been annoyed by her frantic wailing. He had set fire to the woman's field of wheat, mostly because he knew Osiris had visited within the last year, haranguing everyone about the need to cultivate and grow their own food.

Seeing the ripe evidence of Osiris's sad,

pathetic, and, in his opinion, pointless little abilities with plants had angered him, so he decided to burn the field. Perhaps it was out of pettiness, perhaps jealousy. Either way, it would hurt Amun-Ra's favorite golden boy. Also it pleased him to watch all the fleeing animals as they attempted to escape the smoke and flame. Seth liked knowing these sub-creatures feared him and his power. And using his newfound ability to thwart his brother's made him feel right, superior.

Then the woman appeared. She ran from her cottage and fell at Seth's feet, wrapping her thick arms around his legs. Her round face was red and splotchy as she begged him for mercy, asking the "powerful god" to save her husband who was gleaning in the field.

When Seth ignored her and shoved her roughly aside, she exclaimed that he must be the one she'd heard about, the "impotent god." She raised her voice to the sky, keening and crying out to Osiris for help.

That a mortal would dare call him impotent left Seth shocked and, ironically, immobile. But that quickly turned to a fury, which surged through his frame. Any compassion he might have felt for the woman before, as unlikely as it was, melted in the heat of his rage. Seth normally felt next to nothing for the mortal creatures that Amun-Ra and the others always harped on.

With the name of Osiris still on her lips, Seth seized the woman by the throat, lifted her off the ground, and shook her. "You will cease your caterwauling immediately." When she didn't, he threw her on the ground and shouted, "By the gods, I wish the heavens would erase your face from my view!"

Her cries were suddenly cut off and all that could be heard was the bleating of the animals and the crackling of the wheat as it burned. The woman had crumpled to her hands and knees. Her whole body shook but no sound came from her.

Sticking the toe of his boot beneath her bulky form, he thrust her aside and her body rolled away. Seth gasped. Where there had once been a hooked nose, thin pale lips, and eyes that sat too close to one another, he now saw a blank oval. Skin as smooth as a reddening peach stretched where a face should have been.

The woman's hands reached up, clawing, gouging the skin where the mouth and nose once were. But as if a switch had been flipped, her body jolted and then she slumped over, dead. Without a mouth and nose, there was no way for her to take in a breath. Seth lifted his head, shocked and fascinated and sick. *Had he done this?*

Just to make sure, he lifted his hand and stretched it over the woman's foot, willing it to disappear.

Suddenly the foot, including the muddy boot she wore on it, evaporated in thin air, leaving only a stump at the end of her leg. In quick succession, Seth unmade a snake that slithered from the burning stumps of wheat. Several mice disappeared next. Then, he ran, unmaking animals both completely and in parts.

He caused rocks and trees to vanish with the wave of his hand. And, when he came upon the dying form of the burnt farmer, the once husband of the now dead and defaced woman, Seth unmade him bit by tiny bit. He decided to leave only the man's torso and head so he knew exactly how much he could take away from a mortal while still extending their pain-filled life.

Now he was ready. Now he was whole. His power had finally arrived. And it was mightier than he'd ever hoped it would be.

Nothing.

No one.

Could challenge him now.

The world, the cosmos, was ready to be plucked and his first stop was the beauty that haunted him.

Isis was a ripe fruit dangling from a low limb—succulent, juicy, and begging to be consumed. And Seth had never been hungrier.

CHAPTER 1

BUDDING

A horn sounded, its echo filling the hills and valleys surrounding Heliopolis. Isis stood quickly, causing the stool where she'd been sitting at the spinning wheel to topple behind her. The bundle of gray wool in her lap tumbled to the dust. The mortal women surrounding the goddess laughed and clucked their tongues good-naturedly as they picked up the soft mass and shook the dirt from it.

"Go. Go," they admonished, shooing her away. "You'll come back when you can. In the meanwhile, we'll take turns practicing what you've taught us."

Isis gave them a graceful smile and though she attempted to act godlike in her demeanor as she left the village, nodding at the townspeople and patting the heads of the children who always flocked to her, her mind was elsewhere. As a result, her responses were more curt and distracted than usual. The moment she passed the stone wall signifying the border of the town, she shook out her powerful wings and took to the sky.

Energy surged through her body as the golden rays of the sun beat down upon her wings, filling her frame with heat and warmth to the point where she could feel the sting of a blush in her cheeks as well. She laid her hands against them and wondered at the excitement she felt simply because *he* had returned. Her shadow far below flit over the hills and valleys she passed, rising and falling like the tempestuous emotions that seized her mind.

She rose up through the sky, the blue giving way to the black, and she heard the fleeting whispers of the stars welcoming her home. As she passed through the barrier that separated the mortal world from the realm of the gods, speeding through space like a fiery and brilliant comet, the darkness pressed itself upon her. It captured her form, moving her into another dimension. It was quiet in that space and during the transition she gave herself over to her reflections.

It was . . . unfitting, her burgeoning feelings. Isis knew it, but she couldn't help it. And yet, to stifle the way her heart beat with joy at the very thought of him, also felt wrong. Still, Isis had tried to be a proper goddess and ignore her budding affection during the long year of separation when he'd left, taking an assignment elsewhere. But now that he'd returned, she felt the stirring in her heart again and knew that she'd been unsuccessful in uprooting him wholly.

Though Isis had always enjoyed her work—teaching mortals weaving, how to grind corn, and to use plants and herbs to heal—that something else, *someone* else in her life had, of late, occupied her thoughts to the point of distraction. She often caught herself daydreaming or staring at the faraway horizon wondering where he was at that moment and if he was thinking of her as she was thinking of him.

At night, when Isis would slip into her bed, her heavy wings wrapped around her body, she'd catch herself wishing the soft feathers were his arms instead. He'd often done so when they were younger. He'd pin her wings against her body as they played tag, never hurting her, but preventing her from escape until she acknowledged that he'd well and truly caught her. Recently, she'd found herself envisioning the chase once more, but this time, she wanted him to catch her. The thought of what might happen next often left her breathless and sleep would evade her.

Mortal men often fell at her feet, begging for her attention and pledging their undying devotion. Some even dared to reach out and touch her sensitive wings. But at one look from her, they'd drop their hands in fear.

Though a relationship with a mortal was technically allowed, Isis had never found any mortal man who was interesting enough to consider. Besides, the life span of a mortal was like the blink of an eye to a goddess. If she allowed herself to care for a mortal man, she'd watch him grow old and suffer from disease or even the elements.

Isis thought it cruel to tie herself to a mortal. She'd seen Seth toy with the emotions of humans, and it never ended well for them. The lucky ones would pine for him as he disappeared for years at a time. And the unlucky . . . well . . . she didn't want to think about that. Seth had a . . . temper. No. Isis would always be what she was—a goddess. And the love of a goddess was enough to drive a mortal man mad.

Also, there was the fact that as kindhearted as Isis was, she was intimidating. Taller than any human woman she'd ever seen, she towered over most of the men. But her stormy eyes and figure would tempt any mortal. Many of them sought her favor by bringing her carved trinkets or jewels. These she accepted with the airs of a goddess and promised to look after their village or their loved ones in exchange.

But she never encouraged their subtle amorous advances. And any man that proved too bold to be discouraged was sent away. The women who served her made sure those men were banished from her presence, never to press their suit again. Isis by no means ever gave any indication that she was lonely or seeking a companion and yet, as the long years stretched ahead of her, she found she longed for such a thing in the secret places of her heart.

Once, she confessed as much to her soft-spoken sister, Nephthys, the one person she felt truly knew her. Nephthys not only had a very different, much more approachable demeanor than Isis, but they looked as dissimilar as two beings could, despite having the same parents.

It wasn't that Nephthys was ugly. Far from it. She was just small and quiet and so unobtrusive that she was often relegated to the background. But Nephthys was still every inch the goddess. Her long blond hair whispered in the wind like a field of wheat and cascaded nearly to her feet. Delicate silver-tipped delicate wings folded at her back so neatly that they were nearly invisible, and her robin's-egg-blue eyes were lovely.

It was comforting being around her, for she loved absolutely and completely. She was never jealous, cruel, or condescending. Her younger sister saw the good in everyone and everything. No one could listen and empathize as well as Nephthys. To Isis, she was the perfect goddess, who never let troublesome emotions distract her from her duties, and was therefore much more capable than Isis often felt.

Many mortals also disregarded Nephthys, thinking she had no power, but Isis considered her sister's unseen abilities the most potent of all. When Isis first approached her sister regarding her feelings for a true companion, not about any one person in particular, Nephthys listened. She held Isis's hand, her blue eyes wide with understanding and rapt with attention. Nephthys confessed that she, too, had such a desire. Then she said something that shocked Isis, something that she had not forgotten since.

Nephthys leaned forward and said, almost in a whisper, "The stars tell me there is someone meant for you."

"Can it be true?" Isis gripped her sister's hand tightly. "You have seen it?"

"I have," Nephthys responded with a tender smile. "There is much happiness in your future." Then her grin faded slightly.

"And what of you?" Isis asked, wondering what her sister might have seen to cause her sadness. "Will *you* be happy?"

Nephthys sighed faintly. "I will be. Eventually. Unfortunately, trials lie ahead for both of us."

"But where there is love, trials may be endured."

"You are wise, sister."

"As are you," Isis said.

Nephthys nodded shyly, acknowledging the compliment as she hugged her sister tightly, causing their wings to flutter.

Threading her arm through her sister's, Isis rose, and the two goddesses strode through the garden, Isis begging Nephthys for details. "Now, tell me more about this man who will be my true love."

Nephthys laughed and replied, "You know it doesn't work that way with the stars. I cannot see everything."

"Ah, but surely you can tell me something. Is he handsome? Does he have kind eyes? Please tell me he isn't shorter than I am. Is he . . . mortal?"

"No. Not mortal," her evasive sister replied.

The two sisters shared their secret wishes and dreams until Isis sighed and stopped, a frown crossing her face. She took hold of Nephthys's shoulder. "Enough of these imaginings, sister," she said softly. "As much as I would like it to be true, what you say cannot be."

"I tell you it *will* be."

"But the edict. How would such a thing be possible? For either of us?"

Nephthys lifted her head and closed her eyes, breathing in deeply. Isis knew she sought unseen answers. When she opened them, she replied, "I do not know. But the stars cannot lie. What I've seen will be." Offering a small smirk, she added, "Trust in the stars, my beautiful sister."

And Isis did. She went on with her work, at first having an absolute faith in the things her sister had told her. Decades passed, filled with longing and hope. But the more men she met, the more she wavered. Not one of them—mortal or immortal—caught her eye or made her heart flutter with anticipation. Isis began to despair thinking her sister's omen had been wrong. That the stars had deceived Nephthys or that, at the very least, she had misunderstood the signs.

Then one summer night the horns blew, announcing that it was time for the Ennead to gather, a time when all the gods would meet. She hadn't seen him in over a decade but something had changed between them in the time they'd been apart. When he scooped her up and kissed both of her cheeks it felt . . . different than it once had. The warmth of his body seemed to linger, even though he'd left her to embrace Nephthys.

She found herself seeking him out all evening long, and attempted to sit next to him. When that space was already occupied, she fixed her eyes upon him and tried to discern what might have happened to him, what changes had been wrought to make her feel as if she was seeing him for the first time.

Was it the length of his hair? The glow of his skin bronzed by the sun? When he smiled she felt special, as if he were telling her something secretive, somehow meant just for her. When he told stories of his adventures, she wondered if he might be glancing in her direction more frequently than he looked upon the others. By the time the evening festivities were done, Isis knew that the stars had given her the long-awaited gift they'd promised.

The council adjourned, and the one whose attention she sought stretched and rose to retire. Quickly Isis also stood and asked if she might walk with him. He nodded, bright eyes twinkling as he offered her his arm. Together they walked the long halls of Heliopolis, him asking polite questions as they did. All she could focus on was how her heart raced, and Isis wondered if he could feel the thick beat of her pulse where her wrist rested against his muscular arm.

When they reached the wing reserved for her when she was in residence at Amun-Ra's palatial home, he paused and brushed a finger against her cheek. "What is it, Little One?" he asked.

She grinned nervously at his old nickname for her. She'd been taller than him all through their adolescence and "Little One" had been his way of teasing her, but now he easily stood five inches above her, which was no small feat, even for an immortal. Isis had always bristled when he'd called her that before, but the name felt different now. More like an endearment.

"I . . . ," she started to say as she gazed up into his eyes. A fluttery feeling set her nerves on edge and her wings shifted softly behind her. "I missed you," she finally managed to get out.

He laughed kindly. "I missed you, too."

She nodded and lowered her gaze.

Ducking his head, he tried to gauge her expression. "There's something else, isn't there?"

"Yes." A pause, then, "No." Isis wrung her hands and her tongue darted out to lick her lips, her mouth suddenly dry.

He took both her hands in his and gave them a little shake. "Something must truly be upsetting you. I've never known the great goddess Isis to act so flustered."

Isis opened her mouth but couldn't speak.

His gaze narrowed. "Has someone hurt you, Little

One?"

"No. At least, not exactly."

"I see. And who is *not exactly* hurting you?" His eyes had turned cold and flinty, his body rigid. Anger radiated from him.

"It's not a person. It's more of an idea."

That gave him pause. "What do you mean?"

Isis let out a soft sigh, wondering how she was going to explain her feelings. Would he reject her outright? Would he be shocked at her boldness? Or might he, perhaps, be wanting the same thing she did?

She began, "I've been thinking about the laws that govern us, and I find one of them in particular difficult to comply with."

"Which one?"

"The one that says we are not allowed to bind ourselves with another, like Nut and Geb did."

"Ah." He let go of Isis's hands and turned away. With his back straight and stiff, he asked, "So you've found someone you can love?"

"I think so. In truth, I've loved him for many years already."

"I see."

Feeling bold, Isis approached him, opening her wings and wrapping one around him as they stood side by side. She'd often hidden the two of them beneath her gleaming feathers when they were children so they could talk about their plans for mischief making in secret. Now the gesture felt different, new, like she was opening another chapter of her life.

He sighed and turned toward her, his features hidden in the shadow of her wing. "You know the law only applies to immortals, Isis. So there shouldn't be a concern regarding you and your newfound love. Tell me then, what mortal should I be congratulating?"

"I am not in love with a mortal," Isis said.

Cocking his head, he clarified, "Then he *is* immortal?"

"He is. But it's complicated."

"I would say so, although the lines of the law are blurred regarding certain immortals. Your love might still be possible."

"There's another thing. You see, he doesn't know how I feel about him yet."

"Do you doubt that he returns your affection?" He ran a hand through his hair and mumbled, "That was a stupid question. Of course he returns your affection." Lifting his eyes to hers, he touched his fingertips to her jaw. "How could he not?" He gave her a small smile and dropped his hand. He sighed. "I suppose he's handsome."

"Incredibly so."

"Is he kind to you?"

"He has always been kind."

"And he is worthy of you?"

"I can think of no one worthier."

"Then why doesn't he know?"

Isis placed her palm on his shoulder and slid it down the planes of his chest until it covered his heart. "Because he's been gone for a very long time," she voiced quietly.

His brow furrowed and then astonishment ironed out the lines of confusion. "Isis. You cannot mean what you're saying."

"And if I do?"

After cupping her hand with his, he added, with an almost desperate hiss, "Such a thing is forbidden."

"I thought we already talked about that aspect."

"Yes, but . . . this is different. Think of the consequences."

"And what are the consequences of a life lived without love?"

He gently removed her hand from his chest and pressed it between his own. "You can't mean this, Isis. You don't understand."

"I understand loneliness and longing." She brought her other wing around until they stood in the midst of them. "I understand now that it was always you." He swallowed, and when she saw the expression of panic on his face, she took a step back. "Do, do you not feel the slightest bit of affection for me, then?"

In the shadows cast by her wings he took hold of her shoulders and pulled her back. "Isis. Isis, look at me."

When she finally did, he said, "The last thing I want to do is hurt you, but we can't. I can't. No matter what I feel. No matter how strong our bond. It isn't allowed."

Tears filled her eyes. "You . . . you don't, then."

He held her face in his hands, using his thumbs to wipe away her tears, and cursed under his breath. "I'm sorry. You don't know how much I wish . . . Look. You won't be alone. I'll always be with you. I promise you."

"It won't be the same."

"No, it won't."

"I didn't know how painful this would be."

"Then I'll stop talking about what I can't be and tell you what I can be, okay?"

Isis nodded slightly, tears still spilling down her cheeks.

"I can be your friend," he said as he trailed his fingers down a lock of her hair. "I can be your protector." Hugging her close, he murmured in her ear, "I will be your confidant and secret keeper." He kissed her wet cheek. "I'll be your ally." Moving to her other cheek, he added, "I'll be your advocate."

Touching his forehead to hers, he was about to add something else when she interrupted, "But you won't be my beloved."

He froze and stepped back. She lifted her stormy eyes to his, pinning him in place. "We won't seek out stolen moments in your garden or laugh together about memories only the two of us share. We won't tumble in each other's arms as we roll down a hillside. We won't discover together what it truly means to devote ourselves entirely to the well-being of one another. Or understand a love so powerful we're willing to cling to it by our fingertips like Geb and Nut.

"You won't comfort me with kisses or soothing caresses when I'm sad or tired. I won't know that you seek out my face above all others. Or be able to claim you as my own. But worst of all, you won't hold me in your arms every night as we retire together after a long day, a long decade, or a long century of work. You're relegating me, us, to a very long life of limited potential, of not knowing, of undiscovering. So I ask you again, my love, are you sure this half-life is what you want?"

Isis gazed into his troubled eyes and slid her hands around his broad shoulders, threading her fingers together around his neck. Never in her life had she wanted something so badly. Being on the verge of obtaining it, and knowing that it could at any moment be lost to her forever, was a heady, frightening experience—one she'd never had before—and one she wouldn't trade for anything.

Shaking his head slightly, he began, "Isis, I want—" but he cut himself off and just looked at her. What Isis saw in the depths of his eyes made her pulse quicken. Their bodies were locked together. His lips were tantalizingly close to hers.

Held captive by the soft press of her wings against his back and the allure of her lips, he lowered his head to hers and nuzzled her ear, trying desperately to convince himself that he could stop at any time. That he still hadn't gone so far he couldn't pull back. But once he'd caught the scent of her hair, caressed the softness of her skin, and felt the supple length of her body against his, he was lost.

His lips branded a fiery trail from her temple down the curve of her jaw. Isis moaned softly and rocked against him, tilting her head back to grant him access to her throat, closing her eyes to savor the sensation of his lips on her skin. This was what she'd wanted. This was what she craved. A man who would love her wholly and completely. One who would be her companion forever. A man who would share in her sorrow as well as in her joy.

Slowly, achingly, he made his way from her neck back up the side of her face, and just as she was anticipating his kiss, he drew away. The hands that held her trembled. His jaw was set at a hard angle, his mouth in a grim line.

Finally, he opened his eyes. They were filled with pain and regret. "I'm sorry, Little One. You don't know how sorry I am." With that, he spun and disappeared, leaving a cold emptiness where his body had just been.

Isis drew her wings around herself, trying to contain the heat of this passionate moment, but it trickled away until she was left with nothing but loss.

The next morning he was gone.

It had been a year since she'd seen him, a short time by godly standards, but she'd felt each day of separation as if it were a tiny ache carved into her soul. And now he'd returned, and despite everything that had happened, Isis was more certain than ever that the love she felt was real and true. It was a gift from the stars, not to be refuted or squandered.

Isis touched down lightly on the marble balcony and tucked her wings behind her. She raced through the halls and porticoes, searching but not finding, until at last she discovered him. He stood in a room, alone, his back to her as he glanced through Amun-Ra's latest list of concerns and duties.

The sight of him filled her with a strange giddiness coupled with anxiety. She'd waited for him for a long year—the longest one in her memory. And she wouldn't be denied this moment, this reunion. Isis had tamped down the flames of her love until it smoldered slowly, quietly, like hot embers. But seeing him again stoked the fire, reigniting it until it burned hotly in her breast, threatening to incinerate anything that dared to stand in its way.

He must not have heard her approach because he didn't turn, not until she said his name, the name she'd whispered in her dreams.

Osiris.

CHAPTER 2

CULTIVATING

Osiris spun toward her. The papyrus he'd been looking at crackled in his hand from the weight of his fingers tightening around it. "Isis," he said simply.

She took a step toward him but he backed up.

His long legs hit the table, causing it to shift noisily, the grating sound a reflection of the slightly pained expression that crossed his face.

The glow that had come naturally from the happiness she felt upon seeing him slowly melted along with her hope. Clearing her throat, Isis said, "You've returned. Will you be home for long?"

"No," he answered, moving away from her and smoothing the wrinkled papers on the table. "My plan is to leave as soon as Amun-Ra approves the new plans I've designed."

"May I see them?" Isis asked. Her interest was piqued despite the fact that he appeared to be uncomfortable within her presence.

"Surely the great goddess Isis has better things to do than to muck about in the affairs of mortals."

Isis stiffened, her wings rustling in response to her irritation. "And just what is it that you think I do with my time exactly?"

Osiris tilted his head, considering her, and then answered with a deadpan expression, "I don't know. Grow out your hair and then cut it over and over again? Wax your wings, maybe? Fly up into the clouds and make rainbows?"

Her mouth gaped open. but then she noticed the telltale gleam in his eye and the tension she'd felt a moment before ebbed. He was teasing her. Just like he had when they were children. It was nice to know she hadn't lost that part of him. If she couldn't have Osiris in the way she longed to, at least there was a chance she could still keep her close friend.

Isis punched his arm. A gesture she'd made

thousands of times when they were young. "Ruffian," she said, her fond expression still tinged with sadness. "You know me better than that."

"Ow!" he responded with an exaggerated rubbing of his bicep, both of them knowing it would take far more than her fist to hurt him.

"Besides," Isis added, wanting to maintain the ease between them, "my hair is perfect just the way it is."

Osiris laughed fleetingly and caught a strand of her hair between his fingers. "That it is," he answered, his voice low and tender as his eyes lighted on her face. For the tiniest moment, she basked in the warmth of his gaze but it was quickly gone with the clearing of his throat. "Well, if you're sure you want to take a look, help yourself."

After spreading the papers out across the table, he shifted to the side to give her access to them and tried to ignore the brush of her wing against his arm. Osiris knew it would have been smarter to take a step back, to keep temptation far from his reach, but he liked the feel of her soft wings too much to force himself to move. When she exclaimed in excitement over his plans, he actually shifted closer, despite his reservations, peering over her shoulder to see what she was pointing at.

"What do you call it?" she asked.

"I'm thinking about calling it an aqueduct. It's a way for mortals to bring water from lakes and rivers into villages. If they use one, the villagers can build farther away from the river so as not to risk destruction of their homes during flooding season. They will also be able to water crops from a distance. See here?"

He leaned over the table, enjoying the feel of her warm body next to his, and pointed out one section of his drawing. "This can open and close so they can access the water when they wish, and on this side"—Osiris pulled another drawing to the top of the pile—"they can add more sections or move them around depending on what they need the water for. What do you think?" he asked as he stood.

"What do I think? I think it's brilliant, Osiris." Cocking her head to peer up at his handsome face, she teased, "Are you sure you're the one who came up with it?" He laughed as she turned back to his plans and ran her fingertip down the line. "What if you added a siphon?" she said as she tapped the paper. "If the water built up enough speed, it could potentially go over hills, maybe even mountains."

"A siphon? I hadn't considered that." Osiris quickly scribbled some additional notes. The idea had potential. A lot of potential.

"Your mortals will be pleased," Isis said as she straightened and placed a hand on his arm.

Osiris turned toward her and all thought of his new invention fled his mind. He felt something almost tangible pass between them then, something he had no name for. It ebbed and flowed in the space separating them, pulling him gently yet insistently forward. He shifted back, away from her, trying to gain control over his senses once more, and her hand slipped away. Though it was fleeting, he recognized the hint of doubt and sorrow in her eyes. Such an emotion had no place on the face of one as lovely and powerful as Isis. He placed his hands on her shoulders.

"Thank you for the suggestion. I'll see you at the council meeting." With that, Osiris squeezed her shoulders, gathered up his drawings, and left as quickly as his dignity allowed.

* * *

Seth stood in the shadows of the lattice screen where he'd been spying and watched Osiris leave, the plans for his latest scheme clutched in his brother's overly large hands. Now that he considered it, everything about Osiris was large. His body. His overly developed muscles. His ego. His toothy, insipid grin. Actually, the only thing little about Osiris was his intellect. Well, that and perhaps his ambition. Seth snorted. Yes, the dolt aspired to nothing in life except helping mortals. What an absolute waste of time.

If Seth's older brother possessed an ounce of astuteness, he would have noticed the way Isis was, for all intents and purposes, throwing herself at him. Idiot. He didn't know a good thing when it practically pounded down the door and threw itself into his arms. Still, Osiris's failure to see what was right in front of him would work in Seth's favor. His quasi rejection of Isis would make her much more vulnerable. Yes. It was time for Seth to make a move on the delectable goddess.

Seth lifted his own fingers, comparing his long,

lean, and almost delicate hands to Osiris's as he considered his newfound power. He'd been practicing for weeks and hadn't shared his gift with anyone. When he did show the council, he wanted to display his ability on his own terms. He enjoyed imagining the praise he'd get from Amun-Ra and the adoration of all the immortals, especially the females.

But there was one in particular he couldn't wait to share his ability with. When Isis saw what he could do, he was certain she'd fall all over herself trying to gain his attention. She'd want to spend her every free moment with him, not the silly mortals she fawned over. Isis would give heed to his romantic overtures then. The awkward, tight smirk she'd given him before, followed by a rapid disappearance, along with the way her eyes always shifted from him to someone else, anyone else, would be a thing of the past.

Seth's nostrils flared when he remembered how she'd run to Osiris just now. He'd been following her. Watching her. Waiting for the perfect time to reveal himself, his power, and his intentions to take her as his beloved. Unfortunately, it seemed Osiris was now another obstacle he'd have to overcome. But the god of agriculture was no match for him, he sneered. With a simple thought Seth could undo, unmake, every stupid invention Osiris used his peanut-sized brain to conjure. Perhaps someday he'd even risk unmaking the peanut.

Seth wasn't even sure such a thing was possible. Still, the idea of unmaking a god intrigued him. The electric jolt, the infusion of cosmic elements that energized him each time he unmade a being was not something he'd neglected to notice. The more powerful the creature, the more energy he was able to draw into himself. Seth had quickly become addicted to the heady sensation that came with unmaking. He hadn't dared try his new power on anyone who would be missed, let alone on an immortal, but his fingers itched with the desire to try. He couldn't think of anyone he'd rather practice on than Osiris.

Just then, Isis left the room and Seth followed her, keeping to the shadows. If she'd used her abilities she could have discovered him easily, but the gods were complacent. They didn't believe anyone was even capable of thinking ill of them, let alone doing them harm. Isis was as clueless as a newly hatched bird tucked safely in its nest, totally unaware of the snake gazing down upon it contemplating its meal.

Isis wound her way through the gleaming palace Amun-Ra had created until she finally exited and sat down on a marble bench overlooking a park. Young, lesser immortals played in the water fountain, squealing as they ran through the sprays of multicolored water. He wrinkled his nose in distaste.

Seth found the laughter of children an ugly thing. It reminded him of his youth when others had laughed at him during his pathetic attempts to conjure something, anything. Being around the young made his neck feel tight. Tightening his jaw, he indulged his fantasy to commit violence for only a moment and then reined in the very strong desire to unmake every creature in the vicinity. When he was in control, he approached Isis and managed to ignore the flash of discomfort he saw on her face.

"There you are," he said nonchalantly, as if he'd only just happened upon her and hadn't been following her since her arrival.

"Hello, Seth. Are you well?" she asked distractedly.

Beneath the folds of his tunic, he clenched his hands. One day he'd teach her that nothing in this or any world was as important as he was. Outwardly, he was all charm and deference. "Well enough," he said, and then took a page from Osiris's playbook. "I have an idea I'd like to run by you. If you have a moment to spare, that is." Seth's teeth almost ached with the wide leer he gave her. It was an unnatural expression for him.

"Of course," she said. "What is it?"

"I . . ." Seth racked his mind to come up with something, a new invention that would inveigle and impress Isis. When he didn't answer her immediately, she turned her storm-cloud eyes on him fully. He wasn't used to such directness. Most people became uncomfortable and turned away when facing him for more than a few minutes.

Seth knew he wasn't much to look at. Not compared to the other gods. He'd always been tall, but his long limbs were thin, gangly. Only recently, since he came into his power, had he noticed his body filling out. He considered his eyes too watery a blue. His hair too nondescript. And he was cursed with not one, but two cowlicks that made his hair jut up awkwardly no matter how many times he ran his hands through it.

Unlike the other gods, whose skin radiated with

energy and light, his was blotchy and uneven. It was almost as bad as a mortal's. That was probably what he reminded them of. A mortal. Even his own mother, the one person who was supposed to love him unconditionally, wept almost every time they spoke. Her tears rained down upon the Earth until he stood in a sopping mess of her sorrow that he was sure indicated her disappointment in having such a normal sort of powerless man-child for a son.

Then there was the fact that clothing never seemed to fit him properly either. Even animals would run away when they saw him, or worse, would urinate in his path or growl as they peered at him with gleaming eyes in the darkness. Of course, that didn't happen anymore. Strangely, animals seemed to have a sixth sense. They avoided him or slunk away as quietly and as quickly as possible. He rather liked the respect they now showed him. In his opinion, it made them the superior species on Earth.

With Isis's eyes on him, Seth couldn't think, and for a moment he was as tongue-tied as he'd been when he was a youth. She'd always been quicker. Sharper tongued. Isis was always one to compete and had bested him at everything. An idea suddenly came to him. "I've invented a new game. And I'm wondering if you would consider playing it with me tonight."

"A game?" she asked, the delight obvious on her face. Her eyes predictably lit at the idea of a competition. "What do you call it? How do you play?"

"It's called . . . it's called senet," he pronounced, letting the made-up word fall smoothly from his tongue.

"Is it a game of strength, running, or archery?"

"None of those," Seth answered. Of course her mind would turn to the physical (all the easier to best him in that regard). Either that or she was looking for a way to gawk at Osiris flexing his muscles. At the thought, Seth had to consciously control the tremor of irascibility that rose in him. "Senet is a game of wits with a dash of luck."

Isis beamed, and to Seth it appeared almost genuine. This helped to soothe his ruffled feathers. "It sounds like the perfect distraction. When can we play?"

"How about after the council adjourns?"

"Oh." Isis let out a puff of breath. It was obvious she was thinking of something, or perhaps someone, else she could meet with after the council.

"Ah, I see you've already made plans. You are

understandably too busy." Seth stood and adjusted his tunic, pulling it tightly over his narrow shoulders.

"No," Isis said, raising a hand to stop him from departing. "After the council meeting sounds perfect."

Seth gave her a slight bow, and took leave of her then, escaping quickly. There wasn't much time until the feasting would begin. He'd have to use every spare moment to create the game he'd boasted of.

The problem was he wasn't creative enough to come up with something that would impress Isis on his own. He knew creativity wasn't his strength, but he'd wasted a few precious hours trying anyway.

By the time he got to the toy maker's cottage he was sweating profusely, and despite his status as a god, he felt the beginnings of a headache coming on. He ran a hand over his face and grimaced as he felt the patchy bumps of hair. He'd have to shave if he wanted to look presentable for Isis. Then he blinked and attempted to unmake the irritating bristles on his chin and upper lip. Within the space of a second, they'd disappeared. Seth smiled and called out for the toy maker.

He had waited too long. As the old man shuffled into the store, Seth leapt toward him. There was no time for politeness. Seth curled his lip, took the toy maker by the collar, and lifted him off his feet, issuing his demands in as succinct and clear a manner as he could, warning him that there would be dire consequences if he ended up late to the feast.

Then Seth found a spot in the warm cottage and watched the man's still-too-slow progress. When a half hour passed, Seth unmade the man's cat. After another thirty minutes, he unmade a bushel of apples, taking one for himself and munching on it. Then he made a tool disappear and then another. There wasn't much in the room for him to unmake. But Seth soon thought better of disappearing the man's tools. It wouldn't help his cause.

The headache was in full swing after that, and Seth unmade the man's coin purse as well as his wardrobe just because he was hurting. By the time he heard the bellow of the horn announcing it was time to gather, the man thankfully only had one more piece to finish. Seth waited impatiently as the toy maker's shaking hands applied the last coat of paint.

The game pieces were laid inside the wooden box and Seth took it roughly, tucked it under his arm, and prepared to leave. But before he exited, the man spoke up, which was a mistake he wouldn't have the privilege of making again.

"G . . . give the goddess Isis my best," he said. "She helped my wife learn to weave."

Seth turned and bared his teeth in a dangerous sneer. "Oh, I will absolutely give Isis . . . the best. And since you might have reason to cross paths with her, I'd better make sure you won't be distracting her from what's *best.*"

With that, he unmade the toy maker's tongue and hands. It was a shame, since the man obviously had skills, but he couldn't risk the man talking to Isis before Seth was ready. With a mocking salute, Seth left the toy maker's home and headed to the feast with his prize.

CHAPTER 3

BLOOMING

"Baniti, why didn't you call me sooner?" Isis chastised as she took the baby in her arms. The poor thing was so ill that it looked ready to cry, but it couldn't muster the energy to do it.

"You were away," the favorite servant of Isis replied. "I thought it could wait until your return, but he declined so rapidly."

Isis nodded. "I've seen this type of sickness before. It's quick. And deadly," she added. "We must hurry if we're going to save him."

Cuddling the baby close, Isis instructed Baniti to build up the fire while she sang softly to soothe the child. Her wings fanned the air in the small home and the heat radiated around them. Sweat broke out on Baniti's face. The day was already sweltering. To sit in the home with the blazing fire, made even hotter with the power of the goddess, was miserable. The heat was uncomfortable even for Isis herself. But Baniti trusted her goddess. She'd seen her work her magic before, and to great effect. If Isis could save Baniti's little grandson, then she would gladly tolerate a bit of discomfort.

Once the coals of the fire turned white, Isis began weaving her spell. Baniti closed her eyes and whispered, echoing the spell though she possessed no magic of her own. Baniti was so convinced of the goddess's power she didn't even blink an eye when Isis laid her precious grandson directly on the white-hot coals.

The baby screamed, his cries piercing the air. And though Baniti winced, the expression on Isis's face was one of calm determination. The skin on the boy's little arms and legs turned bright red as he kicked and flailed, but Isis remained steadfast, continuing to chant the words of the spell. Steam rose from the baby's body, and when Baniti blinked, the curling wisps seemed almost black as they writhed in the air. They looked as if they were live demons departing the baby's form. Perhaps they were.

Baniti closed her eyes and renewed her chanting with great fervor.

Finally, the baby began to quiet. His glowing skin dimmed until it had returned to its normal color. Sweat trickled from Baniti's temples to her cheeks, and she distractedly swiped at it with the hem of her sleeve. Her fingers itched to pull the baby from the fire, but Isis held out a hand to stop her as if reading her thoughts. "Let me," the goddess said. "The flames will harm you. And he's still too hot from the spell."

Reaching into the crackling flames, Isis picked up the infant and tenderly bathed the ashes from his tiny body. Baniti brought new clothing since the baby's had burned away. When he was dressed, Isis herself having clothed the child, she sat holding him and smiled when he brought his thumb to his mouth. "He is whole again," Isis said. "The disease was purged from his body. My magic will protect him from its effect for the remainder of his life."

Tearfully, Baniti knelt at the goddess's feet and placed her palm on her grandson's forehead. "Thank you," she said.

Isis shifted the baby to one arm and stroked the

old woman's cheek. "It is I who should thank you. You have been of great comfort to me over these long years. I am glad to have been able to offer you some of the same."

Isis whispered a word to bank the fire, then lifted her wings and stirred the air around the child, gently cooling him. The two women were quiet for a moment as they listened to the baby suck on his thumb. "You're good with him," Baniti said, rising with a groan. "If only—"

"It is not meant to be," Isis interrupted quickly, already knowing what Baniti was going to say. She frowned watching Baniti struggle to her feet. Seeing one she loved so enfeebled saddened her. "We've had this discussion before," Isis finished distractedly.

"But surely Amun-Ra can—"

"Even if he could, he wouldn't." Isis stroked the downy head of the newborn.

"Besides, for a child to even be a possibility, there would have to be a man in my life first. And the one I'm interested in is more concerned with duty than love."

"So there *is* someone. I have to admit, I've been wondering about you. Will you tell me who he is?"

Isis sighed. "It doesn't matter. He isn't receptive."

"Then he's a fool."

"Be that as it may, Amun-Ra has always told us to content ourselves with what we are and that the state we are born into is the only state we should aspire to. Even if the one I wanted desired me in return, his adherence to the law is firm. It seems I should relegate myself to a life lived alone."

"Bah," Baniti said with a dismissive wave of her hand and bustled about the small home straightening the baby's things as she waited for his mother to return from the fields. "No one deserves to be alone. Especially one such as you. I don't believe Amun-Ra's opinion is valid."

"No?"

"Absolutely not. If we mortals had nothing to aspire to, we'd just give up and die in our beds. There is no reason you can't seek out what you dream. Everyone has the right to dream of something more."

"Perhaps you are right." Isis kissed the little cheek of the sleeping baby and handed him to Baniti, who settled him in his basket and tucked his blanket around him. "I must return to the council."

Baniti took Isis's hand, cupping hers around it. Very few mortals dared to touch the goddess, but Baniti had been hers ever since Isis found her as an abandoned child. The goddess was like a mother to her, though now Baniti looked the part of the goddess's great-grandmother. "Isis, if a love of your own and a child by that man is the secret wish of your heart, then you will make it happen. Trust in yourself and your power. I always have."

Isis wrapped her arms around the old woman and was shocked at how slight and fragile her frame was. Baniti shuddered and coughed, seemingly unable to catch her breath. Several moments passed until Baniti was able to breathe normally again. Isis, who had taken hold of her shoulders during her struggle, asked, "Is it the same sickness as the child?"

Baniti shook her hand and coughed again before answering. "No, goddess. The tickling of my lungs is different."

"Why didn't you tell me?"

She shrugged. "I'm an old woman. Do you think I'll live as long as you?"

"You're not old." Isis shook her slightly and then stopped, remembering how frail the woman was now. "You're still young," she said, denying the obvious. "It wasn't that long ago we were running and playing together."

"That was decades ago."

Kissing Baniti's wrinkled forehead, Isis admonished, "Shhh. Remain still."

Isis moved behind her beloved servant and pressed her hands against the woman's back. She could feel the fluid filling her lungs, making her breathing difficult. The goddess attempted to use a spell to heal her, but Baniti's aging form rejected her magic. It was the way of things. Each being in the universe was allotted a certain portion of time, a span for them to live their lives. Once that time ran out, there was nothing anyone, not even the gods, could do to prevent it from fading. She knew it, but it was too soon. Isis staggered back, her eyes filling with tears. "No," she whispered. "I'm not ready to let you go."

"You might not be ready, but I am. This body isn't strong anymore. When I'm awake, I hurt. When I lie down, I ache. There's no rest for me."

"I'll fix this," Isis promised. "You aren't going to die before the next moon. That much I can tell. But this sickness will weaken you. It will bring you to the door of death if I don't find a way to do something about it."

"Then maybe it's time to introduce me to that good-looking Anubis. I can think of worse ways to go than to be escorted to the afterlife on the arm of one such as him."

"I don't think so. I'm keeping you far away from Anubis."

"What a pity," Baniti said and when she saw Isis still hesitating she waved her arms.

"All right, all right, now shoo. Go on to your meeting. I'll be here when it's over."

"Yes, you will," Isis said with determination.

Patting Baniti's arm in farewell, Isis leapt into the air, her wings snapping open to carry her back to the barrier between the mortal realm and Heliopolis.

* * *

"No," Amun-Ra said after Isis asked again, begging him with all the sincerity of her soul and even offering a part of herself. "You know it isn't allowed, there just isn't enough life energy remaining in the Waters of Chaos. Besides, mortals are what we've created them to be. Unfortunately, the very definition of *mortal* is that death is inevitable."

"But don't you see? It doesn't have to be. These rules are self-imposed. Surely there can be exceptions."

"Then when do we stop, Isis? Which god will you take energy from to make her immortal? Nut? Geb? Because that's what would have to happen. And if I allowed you to use a part of your own power, there would soon be nothing left of you. You love your mortals too much. I cannot risk such a thing. Surely you understand the ramifications. The entire cosmos could implode!"

"But we don't know that, do we?"

He sighed and sat back in his chair. "It's better to be safe, Isis. We must keep our creations safe and keep our family safe. When we play with dangerous substances, we ensure our own destruction."

"But what if there was another way?" She hadn't considered it before, but the idea had come to her when a bird flew past the window overhead.

"And what way would that be?"

"What if I took the life energy of another creation? Not a god, but perhaps an ancient tree or an animal?" she suggested. Even as she spoke, the words of a spell, a powerful one, filled her mind. She could do it. She knew she could.

Amun-Ra interrupted her thoughts. "And why does the animal or tree deserve to give over its existence to prolong the life of another?"

"We could ask it to volunteer."

"No," he answered, forming his lips around the word in such a way that she knew he would brook no further argument.

Isis threw up her hands and growled, "You're not keeping an open mind."

"And I'd say *your* mind is *too* open. What you're suggesting is an abuse of our powers."

"Amun-Ra is right, Isis," a familiar voice interrupted.

Stiffening, Isis turned away from the man who'd entered the chamber. "This is a private conversation, Osiris."

"I'm sorry if I've come at an inopportune time, but I overheard what you said and felt I should caution you that the others would be milling about here soon. Perhaps this conversation would best be held in another place? A place not easily accessed by the entire Ennead."

Isis folded her arms and frowned, finally looking at Osiris. Seeing the I'm-much-wiser-than-you, big-brotherly expression of tolerant pity on his face was the last straw. She was about to light into him when Amun-Ra held up a hand. "Thank you for the timely interruption, Osiris. He is right that we need to turn our attention to other things at present. I'm afraid this is my final decision, Isis. I warn you that no amount of pleading or abasing is going to change my mind. I'm sorry. Now please excuse me as I take my leave to make sure the feast is prepared."

As Amun-Ra swept from the room, all the fight went out of her, leaving a brokenhearted Isis alone with Osiris.

"For what it's worth, I'm sorry," he said.

She sniffed. "You don't even know what you're sorry for."

"I'm sorry for a lot of things where you're concerned, actually. Despite that, he's right. We have laws for a reason."

"I don't want to talk to you about laws."

"Well, too bad."

Isis was startled at his tone. Osiris had never been anything but polite and patient with her. He raked a hand through his dark hair. "Look, I understand having an attachment, even one that's . . . deeply felt, but there's something to be said for controlling ourselves. There must be moderation. Adhering to the statutes Amun-Ra put in place is not a bad thing."

"But what if there's more?" she challenged.

"What? What do you mean?"

"If by our laws we are bound, then perhaps by breaking them we are boundless," replied Isis.

"You're not making any sense."

"What I mean is that the very things that weaken us, that cause us to feel . . . vulnerable"—Osiris raised an eyebrow—"might actually make us more powerful than we could possibly imagine," she finished.

He sighed. "Isis—" he began, but she cut him off with the wave of her hand.

Locking her eyes to his, she challenged, "What if there was a way for us to fulfill our dreams? To have what we most desire, simply by embracing the things that outwardly appear unsuitable?"

She took a step forward, the tree branches in the atrium casting their grayish-blue shadows over her face. Osiris edged back nervously. Isis pressed on trying to explain it in a way Osiris would understand. "Why should we be satisfied with a simple harvest, an acceptable yield, when we have the ability to produce more?"

Osiris knew very well that Isis was no longer

talking about saving her mortal. At least, that wasn't the only thing she was alluding to. The fact that her words echoed the little voice in his mind, the one he'd been trying to ignore, didn't help. He couldn't, wouldn't consider what she was asking. It would undo everything. Cold fear crept through his veins.

He stared at her as if she'd lost her mind. It roused her temper. Irritated, she continued, "If it was possible for you to achieve something, to attain something, to aspire to something you yearned for above all else, wouldn't you give anything just to have the opportunity? Why do we have all this power, Osiris, if we aren't meant to use it?"

A clapping sound echoed in the room. "Hear, hear. I wholeheartedly agree with you, Isis."

Osiris frowned at the new arrival. "Seth. We are in the middle of a private conversation."

"How ironic for you to adopt that attitude, Osiris," Isis said, her irritation turning into ire. "It matters not, regardless. I can see your mind is fixed upon your course of action. This discussion is over."

Isis swept around Osiris as he stood rooted in place, and his back stiffened as he heard Seth ask if he could escort Isis to the feast. He had been meaning to accompany her himself, as a sort of peace offering between them. By doing so, he'd been hoping to make amends for the poor way he'd handled her before. In truth, he'd been able to think of little else but her when he was gone. Coming home had been an excuse. Osiris wanted to fix what was wrong between them and now Seth was getting in the way.

When Isis agreed to sit next to Seth at the feast as well, Osiris tightened his hands into fists and trailed slowly behind them, never taking his eyes off Isis's gleaming wings except to glare at Seth's hand that had encircled her waist.

His mood didn't improve during dinner. Seth had positioned himself near the head of the table in the spot usually reserved for Osiris. Then he somehow managed to have Isis sit on one side of him and Nephthys on the other. He also caught Seth sneaking looks at Isis whenever her attention was turned to something else. Was it possible that Seth was interested in her in a romantic way?

Osiris wouldn't put it past him. Seth was never one to take rules too seriously. Isis was lonely. She wanted someone to love her, to offer her more than just friendship. Then there was the undeniable fact that Isis was the loveliest creature he'd ever seen. Surely Osiris wasn't the only man who'd noticed her.

None of them, not even Isis, had ever taken Seth seriously before. He was always tagging along, trying to keep up with the other gods. Osiris rubbed his jaw as he studied Seth. The boy had filled out a bit, but he was still rough around the edges. Seth had always been wild, angry. He'd treated mortals badly, demanded their adoration. Osiris didn't want that for Isis. She deserved much better than Seth.

When Seth offered Isis a berry and nudged the succulent fruit between her lips himself, Osiris could not control the shaking of his hands. He tried to talk about something else, anything else, to distract himself from the scene being played out in front of his eyes. But his reports on vegetation, crops, and the wonders of nature weren't enough to take his attention away from Seth's obvious flirtation. How could no one else be noticing Seth's behavior? Was he always like this now?

Seth even began charming Nephthys. The man had no shame. As he sat at dinner gloating over his latest exploits, each astounding achievement questionable at best, everyone turned a rapt ear. How could they believe that Seth rescued an entire village from a fire? Seth had never lifted a finger to help anyone, especially mortals. Even Osiris couldn't help but listen and gape at the man's audacity as he spoke of returning stolen infants to parents, encouraging misguided youth, and even rescuing a nest of baby birds from the mouth of a hungry viper.

Seth kissed Nephthys's hand in an all-too-friendly manner and promised she could play the winner after he challenged Isis to the new game he'd invented. A game. Osiris snorted in disgust. Surely there were better uses of a god's time than games.

Wanting to distract himself from the distasteful display Seth was orchestrating, Osiris attempted to wipe the sullen expression from his face. He then cleared his throat and said, "I have an interesting story to share."

Though all eyes turned toward Osiris, Isis lifted her cup and pointedly looked away, ignoring him. Seth noticed and curled his lips in a mocking grin. "Tell us, then," Seth said. "For I personally find farm tools and the merits of various types of manure vastly interesting," he finished with a sweeping gesture of his arm.

Osiris tried to ignore him and said, "A farmer told me that an enemy had come upon his field by night and had sown tares among his crop of wheat. There was no way to know it had happened until the grain started to grow and the tares became obvious."

"Fascinating," Seth said with a pinched mouth, then laced his fingers together and rested his chin upon them. "Do go on."

"He asked me if he should remove the tares immediately, but I cautioned him not to, saying that if he removed them early, it might damage the wheat. I instructed him to wait until they were grown and then harvest the wheat and burn the tares." Osiris leaned forward, pressing his hands against the table. "The funny thing about tares is that when the seedlings are young, they look just like the wheat. But they are nothing like the plant they mimic."

Osiris looked around the room. "Tares have no purpose. They have no value. They take up precious space in an otherwise fertile, productive field. They do not serve mankind. In fact"—he turned his eyes to Seth and narrowed his eyes—"they are nothing more than a blight to be rooted out and burned."

Seth wrenched back in his chair, the expression on his face volatile. "Then perhaps the thing to do would be to burn the whole field," he spat.

"That would be wasteful, don't you think?" Osiris answered as he folded his arms across his broad chest.

"Well, I guess that's the difference between you and me," Seth answered. "I wouldn't waste time trying to salvage a few scrawny stalks of wheat when I can just raze the crop and start over again."

"Perhaps you're right," Osiris acceded. "It would be easier. But the easiest path is not always the best one. Struggle often strengthens."

"An interesting debate, to be sure," Amun-Ra said with a quick glance at Nephthys, "but I'm more interested in music at present." The staunchly neutral diplomatic leader of the gods pressed on, insisting they change the subject in his own way. "Osiris, what musicians have you brought us this time?"

Osiris reluctantly drew his eyes away from Seth. "Ah, yes, I nearly forgot. On my last journey I came across two men who have created an instrument they call a sistrum."

The table was cleared as the musicians set up. Osiris couldn't help but be pleased when he overheard Seth trying to spirit Isis away for the promised game, but she waved her hand, saying that she'd meet him after the musicians were finished. Then his rising confidence took a hit when she added that the music was what she enjoyed the most about having Osiris visit. When Seth whined, trying to manipulate her into doing what he wanted, Nephthys volunteered to play him first.

It was clear that Seth was undecided, so to help him move along, Osiris approached and bowed briefly to Isis. "I was wondering if I could entice my . . . my dear *friend* to a dance?"

Isis glared at Osiris, obviously still upset about his siding with Amun-Ra, if not about other things. She replied a bit coldly, "I wouldn't know. Do you *have* any friends here?"

Seth chortled in delight. "Come, Nephthys, my dear. We'll return for Isis later." He brazenly stroked Isis's silky wing. "Don't be too long," he said. "I've been looking forward to besting you in this game."

Osiris clenched his fists and frowned.

"I'd offer to play you," Seth said to Osiris, "but I'm afraid it might be a little bit over your head," he teased with pinched fingers, trying to indicate the size of Osiris's intellect.

Osiris itched to bang Seth's head against the wall but somehow managed to restrain himself. "Move along and play your little games, Seth. Some of us have more important things to do."

Seth's calculating eyes turned sharp, dangerous, but Nephthys quickly whispered something in his ear. It must have been an effective distraction, because the two of them soon left. Since Isis was ignoring him, Osiris turned his attention to the musicians as their music swelled, filling the halls of Heliopolis.

When they finished a series of merry tunes, one of the musicians lifted his eyebrows toward Osiris. He nodded, acknowledging the request, and when the new song began, his voice rose in accompaniment.

Isis closed her eyes and rocked slightly, her wings quivering as every nerve in her body seemed to hum along in response. Her voice was powerful when it came to weaving spells, but no one could best Osiris in weaving songs. He sang of snowcapped mountains and valleys of recently tilled black soil waiting to be planted. Of hills covered with sweet blue grass and of waterfalls that plummeted so far, the water dissipated into clouds on the way down.

She was so caught up in the notes and the words; Isis knew she could glide forever on the current of his music. She let Osiris's voice buoy her up until the end, when he'd set her feet gently back on the ground before sweeping her away into the next song. His music filled her with peace and, at the same time, unrest. With a deep satisfaction and with a terrible longing. The wanting was never so powerful as when he sang.

When he pulled her into his arms, it felt natural. They'd danced together a thousand times, but this time was different. It was new. She felt the song flow through him into her. The words he sang now were quiet and gentle but deeply felt. He sang of unspoken wishes and heartache. Of places he hadn't yet seen and of those imagined things so beautiful he couldn't find the words because describing them would somehow diminish the dream.

She'd kept her eyes closed as they moved together, and only at the end of the song did she realize how badly her limbs were shaking; Osiris was supporting most of her weight. He didn't seem to mind, though, and as a new song began, this time without his vocal accompaniment, Osiris pulled her close. "Will you walk in the garden with me?" he asked softly.

Silently, she nodded and he took her arm, tucking her hand into the crook of his elbow. They walked in silence, and Isis was suddenly acutely aware of everything: the rustle of her wings; the feel of his arm; the way his hand cupped hers almost possessively, as if he was trying to prevent her escape; the troubled, almost determined expression on his face; and then, when they got close enough, the smell of the flowers wafting from his garden.

Osiris was fiercely proud of his enchanted garden. Even when he was abroad, plants of all description were sent via messenger with explicit instructions for their care. He employed a whole staff of gardeners who cultivated and labeled each specimen, placing it in the proper location where it would thrive. Because of this, the vast area had been divided into several zones.

One almost desertlike environment housed the various slow-growing plants he called succulents. Another was devoted solely to herbs and vegetables, most of which were shared with the citizens of Heliopolis. There was an orchard that grew hundreds of different summer fruits. Acres were dedicated to the climbing vines.

Bushes as tall as homes grew fat berries of all colors. A section was dedicated to plants that grew in cold climates, and Amun-Ra had graciously provided the means to keep that area cool for centuries. The tropical plants were kept on the opposite side of the garden. There were greenhouses, shadehouses, and a giant arboretum with every kind of tree grown on Earth and on the other worlds they'd seeded.

Isis loved the garden and often visited it when Osiris was away. She felt close to him when she was there, but like him, she was drawn to the mortals. There were many who could see to the needs of the plants, but few who had the ability to travel to the mortal realm as they did and care for the people there.

She was surprised and happy when he brought her to a grove of nut trees. A cozy gazebo was tucked in the center. It was a place he'd had built for her when she was young. He gestured that she should take a seat and made sure she was comfortable before walking away. She stared at his back and wondered what troubled him so. That he was upset was obvious, but from her perspective, she should be the one angry with him, not the other way around.

"What is it, Osiris?"

He clasped his hands behind his back and turned his head so she could see his handsome face in profile. The sun had already set, and now the moon was rising, framing him in its orb and gilding the tips of his dark hair silver. Finally, he shifted, leaning back against a post. Folding his arms across his chest, he perused her from the shadows. He worked his jaw as if almost starting to speak, but then stopped himself as if he couldn't trust his own voice.

"Are you angry with me?" she asked.

"Angry?" Osiris echoed. The word puzzled him. It tasted thick and wrong on his tongue. "No. I'm not angry with you." What he felt for Isis had nothing to do with anger, though the heat of such an emotion did burn within him. As he looked at her, dazzling in the light of the moon, he considered her the way he did when he came across a rare and most beautiful flower.

The delight he experienced at finding such a thing was almost heady and it filled him with euphoria. He'd cup the blossom between his hands and inhale its delicate scent. Then he'd study it and its surroundings. Carefully and painstakingly he'd watch over it for an entire life cycle taking copious notes, and then, when he was finally ready to take possession of it, he'd bring it home to the perfect spot and lavish all his attention on it until it thrived under his care.

That was what he longed to do when he looked at Isis. He wanted to cup her exquisite face in his hands and figure out what she needed, how he could make *her* flourish. Of course Osiris couldn't say such a thing to her. Not without consequences. He knew her well enough to know she couldn't just take such an admission into her heart and store it away. No. She would want to act upon it, and he could not allow that to happen.

While he worried over these things, Isis rose from her seat and approached him. In her eyes, he could see the eternity of the cosmos, the birth of stars, the churning of nebulas. They transfixed him, cast a spell upon him, and he felt intoxicated by the moonshine reflected in them. But that didn't matter. He needed to tell her what he'd come to say. "Seth . . . overreaches," he said finally.

"Seth?" she questioned, a look of puzzlement on her face. "Why do you speak of Seth?"

"He wants something from you."

She lifted a shoulder, as if she gave no thought to

the matter. "Seth has always sought our approval."

"No. This is different. He . . . he desires you."

Isis frowned. "I think you are mistaken."

"I am not. Do you think I cannot discern when a man wants a woman?"

"I did not think you cared to notice such things."

"In your case, I do."

Tilting her head, Isis considered his words. "I see." Then she nodded. "Thank you for making me aware of it."

She made as if to leave, but Osiris took hold of her arm to draw her back. "I . . . I need to know. What do you intend to do about it?"

"About Seth?"

Osiris inclined his head and held his breath for her answer.

It was a full three heartbeats until she spoke. "I suppose I'll need to talk with him about it."

"Ah." Osiris let go of her arm and sucked in a breath. "But . . . but what do you plan to say?"

She shifted uncomfortably. "I don't know. I'll consider his words first and then make a decision. There isn't much for me to do unless he declares his intentions."

"Right."

This time she did turn to go and Osiris hurried to block her path before she exited, taking hold of her shoulders. "Don't," he said. "Just . . . don't."

"Don't what? Leave? Talk to Seth? Walk home? What *don't* you want me to do?"

"Don't consider him."

"And why not?"

"You know why not."

"Your reasons are not the same as mine."

"They should be."

"But they are not," she answered, her chin lifted defiantly. "You cannot make my decisions."

"Perhaps not, but I *am* affected by them."

"How so?"

"If you choose him, I will . . . suffer."

"Yet *you* still refuse me, do you not?"

"That is correct."

"Then you want *me* to suffer instead."

"No. That's not—" He sighed. "I don't want you to suffer, Isis. It's just . . . Seth isn't right for you."

"Then who is?"

Osiris chose not to answer her. Instead, he took a

step closer, cupped her cheek, and stroked her soft skin with his thumb. Soothingly , he murmured, "You are as delicate and lovely as a moonbeam." Bringing his other hand to her face, he traced the line of her jaw. Giving in to temptation, he drew her close, relishing the feel of her palms on his chest. Then he leaned down and whispered in her ear, "I would not have Seth tarnish your light."

Isis slid her hands up and twined her arms around his neck before saying, "Then give me another option."

Before Osiris could respond, Isis lifted her mouth to his, and all thoughts of what he was going to say escaped his mind. When she angled her head and pressed closer, he groaned and wrapped his arms tightly around her waist, actually lifting her from the ground. Her wings fluttered, and a part of him was aware that he was no longer holding her weight. Then she tucked her wings and fell against him once more and he thought nothing in his life had ever felt so good, so right, as holding the weight of her in his arms.

Isis was the brightest star in the cosmos. And she was his for the taking. He was caught in her orbit and he'd burn up in her presence. But he didn't care. He *wanted* this. He wanted *her*. More than he'd ever wanted anything since his life began. And yet, he knew he couldn't have her.

Gently, he set her down and stepped back. The cruel distance separating them was like a living thing taunting him just after they'd been violently ripped apart. Her eyes were soft, shining. Packed with promises.

The lips he'd just kissed were full and lush and tempting and it would be so easy to lower his head and taste them again. The slow smile that built as she lifted a hand to stroke his hair was heartbreaking, and he knew the becoming flush of her cheeks was something he'd treasure for the rest of his days.

Capturing her hand, he brought it to his lips and pressed a tender kiss on her palm. "I'm sorry," he said. It was a pathetic echo of what had happened between them before. But that time he'd been running from the consequences of what she'd proposed. This time he was running from his own feelings. And there was no denying it now. The feelings he had for Isis were very real. The only question was what he would do about them.

"What?" she asked, blinking back in confusion.

"I said I'm sorry, but I need to go."

"Go?"

"Yes. I need to think."

He quickly headed down the gazebo steps and onto the moonlit grass.

"Think?" she cried out, obviously upset. "By all means then, run away and *think,* Osiris! But just be warned that I plan to do a lot of *thinking* myself!" With that, Isis leapt from the gazebo, opened her wings with a snap, and disappeared into the starry night.

From the shadows of a tree, Seth watched, eyes glittering as Isis took to the sky and Osiris stormed off. Things were not proceeding as planned, but Seth thought he might still be able to turn them in his favor.

CHAPTER 4

GRAFTING

The easiest way to thwart their burgeoning relationship would be to approach Amun-Ra. Seth rubbed his jaw. No. Reporting their activities would hamper his own agenda. If he was going to bind Isis to himself, he needed to keep Amun-Ra as ignorant as possible about Isis's current feelings of wanting something more than she was allotted.

In truth, that was something Seth admired about her. In a way, it was a relief to know that she was just as discontented with her lot in life as he was. Spying on her was useful in more ways than one. He could use that to his advantage. Seth spent the entire night rehearsing what he would do and say to sway Isis. To have Isis look at him as a more viable choice than Osiris. Then, as the sun rose over the mountain, casting all of Heliopolis in its golden glow, he called to his mother, asking if he could borrow her comet to send a message.

The sky rumbled in response and the whisper of wind tickled his cheek. "I would," Nut said to her son, "but Osiris asked for just the same thing before you did. When the comet returns, I would be happy to pass along a message for you."

Seth clenched his fist as his jaw tightened. "That won't be necessary, Mother," he snapped. He then quickly apologized, explaining that he was wearied, and added, "Did you happen to overhear his message?"

"You know I don't listen in on my children."

"So you don't know what he said to her?" Seth pressed.

The wind stilled, and then stirred around his feet so subtly that if he hadn't been a god, he wouldn't have noticed it at all. "It was not meant for you, son," he heard her softly admit.

Seth's body shook with frustration. "Could you not this once . . . ." he began, struggling to show his mother the respect her position demanded. Nut interrupted with a sudden stir of the clouds overhead. They roiled and churned, but as quickly as they had formed, the thick mass broke apart. It stretched out thin fingers that dissipated in the heat of the morning sun until they were gone.

"I don't normally do this," she said finally, "but I know you've had a difficult time of late, and the other gods haven't been as patient with you as I wish they'd be." She sighed. Her breath on his face was as cold as the space in which she made her home. "Osiris has asked Isis to meet him at the stables of Amun-Ra. I do not know if she intends to go, only that the message was delivered."

Seth inclined his head. "Thank you, Mother."

On his way to the stables Seth was stopped twice, first by Anubis. "Seth," Anubis said. "Just the boy I've been looking for."

Seth wrenched his arm from Anubis's grip and glared at the god with open contempt. "I don't see any *boys* here. You'd best keep looking." He turned to go, but Anubis's black dog leapt in his path and growled. Almost, *almost,* he unmade the dog then and there. Unmaking a creature as ancient as the first dog would imbue him with a great deal of power, but he couldn't risk such a thing. Not yet. Without turning to look at him, Seth asked, "What do you want, Anubis?"

"It seems that there have been some interesting deaths as of late—animals, trees, mortals, and even some of the lesser immortals as well. I've had to escort several people to the afterlife, several *young* people," he emphasized. "Youth who weren't remotely close to death. And the stories they tell, well . . ." Anubis had repositioned himself alongside his dog and peered into Seth's face with his not-so-subtle accusations. "Let's just say they weren't entirely . . . *natural.*"

"How fascinating that must be for you. Now if you'll excuse me, I have pressing business."

Anubis lifted an eyebrow. "Business? Really? What business could you possibly have?"

Seth raised his chin and narrowed his eyes. "I'll have you know that Amun-Ra has sent me out on a mission of great import."

Anubis folded his arms across his chest. "I see. Well, lucky for him he has such a dedicated *man* to do the job."

"Yes."

"Best move along then, Seth." The god of the afterlife smirked. "I'll just go speak to Amun-Ra about my concerns regarding the sudden influx of souls to the afterlife and my *suspicions* as to what has caused them."

"You do that," Seth said confidently, despite his inner turmoil that his secret had been discovered. Then he calmed himself. Even if Anubis suspected him in the deaths, Amun-Ra wouldn't necessarily attribute them to the supernatural. He'd caused mortal death before—many deaths, in fact.

Anubis might believe these deaths were different, but he couldn't know why. The transition between life and death was a terrible enough thing that the mind encapsulated the pain of it. Most souls couldn't even remember how they died. It was like remembering the pain of a skinned knee as a toddler. Even if they could, it wouldn't be an immediate concern. He'd been careful to make sure the mortals he tested his power on never saw his face. Besides, they were more focused on the next phase of their existence and their upcoming judgment. At best the mind was clouded, confused about the experience of dying, which was why Anubis was often sent as a guide.

For the time being, his secret was safe. No one would believe that the one god without power, the one nobody, including his parents, thought would amount to much, could possess such an important ability. There was still time. Time for him to reveal his news in his own way and to those he sought out. But first, he needed to get to Isis.

Anubis leaned forward, almost touching his nose to Seth's. "Oh, I will," he breathed before he walked past him, knocking into Seth's shoulder so hard that the shorter god almost fell. The fury that swept through Seth was quick and burning. Mostly he was angry at how Anubis had spoken to him, but he was also upset with his own reaction to the god. During their conversation Seth had felt . . . intimidated, fearful, and less-than.

He hated that the old inadequacies of his youth still plagued his mind, even though he'd now come into his own. How he ached with righteous vengeance. He would show them. He would show them all just what he was. What he could be. He was more powerful than all of them. They wouldn't dare talk to him like that after they saw what he could do.

Seth stormed off, once again headed to the stables,

but then he ran into Nephthys, who also clearly desired his attention. At first, he thought to ignore her, but her soft eyes and demure smile charmed him. Though Nephthys had always grouped herself with the others, leaving him out, she'd never been unkind to him. Stifling his impatience, he feigned interest in whatever it was she wanted to talk to him about. "What can I help you with, my dear?"

She wrung her hands. "I . . . I've been speaking to the stars."

"Yes?" The others thought Nephthys a touch mad when she spoke of her visions, but Seth always took what she said seriously. He knew what it was like to be misunderstood, and now that he thought about it, they had much in common. Her abilities frightened the others. When he revealed his, they would be equally concerned, if not more so. "What did the stars tell you?" he asked.

"I'm to warn you."

"Warn me of what?"

"That the path you're taking is a dangerous one."

Seth laughed. "My path to the stables?"

"No. Your life path."

"I see. And what would the correct path be?" At

first he meant the question as a joke, but the tone of her voice coupled with the expression on her face twisted inside him; he now earnestly wanted to know.

Nephthys pulled a clear stone from her pocket and rubbed her fingers over it. She then cupped it in her hands and held it up to her ear. "There are several you could take," she said. "Your path has so many twists and turns. So many possibilities. And an important choice comes soon."

"What is that?" he asked, pointing to the stone.

The corner of her mouth quirked up. "You wouldn't believe me if I told you."

Seth leaned in, took hold of her shoulder, and squeezed, trying to evoke an air of confidence between them. Winking, he said, "Try me."

Wetting her lips, Nephthys answered, "I call it the Eye of Prophecy. When the messages from the stars are unclear, I set it to wandering. It's recently returned, and the things it's shown are both wonderful and frightening."

"Will it speak to me?" Seth asked, opening his hand. When she hesitated, he pried the stone from her fingers and lifted it to his ear. That she didn't seem to mind his taking the stone filled him with a heady sense of power. It was exactly the opposite of what he'd felt during his encounter with Anubis.

Seth didn't know if she was charmed by him, fearful of him, or was just being polite. It didn't matter really what her motivation might be. That she knew her place made him appreciate her all the more. Briefly, he wondered just how much Nephthys would allow him to push her.

"No." Nephthys shook her head sadly. "I wish it would. There's so much to tell you. So much you need to know. But . . . the time isn't right."

"How convenient," Seth said, allowing a glimmer of his cruelty to show. When he saw her fallen expression, it made him angry. He didn't like when people were disappointed with him. "Don't bother me with such things if you don't have anything concrete to share."

"But I do have something concrete."

"Then say it, Nephthys," he demanded impatiently.

"It's about your path." She lowered her eyes. "I mean, *our* path." She swallowed and peeked up at him through her lashes.

"Our path?" Seth said with a start. "Do you mean

to tell me that we . . . ?"

Nephthys nodded slightly. "It is one of the possibilities. One of the happier ones." She frowned. "But also one of the terrible ones."

Seth stood frozen, his hands now gripping her shoulders. He'd never considered taking a woman other than Isis as his companion, but standing there with Nephthys looking at him with a mixture of trust and fear felt somehow right. There was no doubt in his mind that Nephthys's power was real. She knew too many things.

It reminded him of his mother in some ways. But unlike his mother, Nephthys at least trusted him enough to tell him of the things she'd seen. Nephthys didn't hold back. Even if what she told him was met with anger. He took a moment to consider what she'd said. That he had the potential for many paths was a good thing. It meant he had choices. That fate hadn't decided who or what he was to be. He liked that.

Perhaps her visions even meant that he could have both women—one to cast his spells and one to see the future. A man could do much worse. And wouldn't the other gods be jealous at seeing him toy with the affections of both goddesses while they all remained steadfastly alone? Old bachelors doomed to a life of envy? He imagined the handsome Osiris kneeling before his throne, gazing jealously upon him as his powerful queens sat one on each side competing for his attention. It was a dream potent enough that Seth could almost taste it.

Whether he chose Nephthys now or later was immaterial to him. It couldn't hurt to keep the goddess on a baited hook for a few centuries. At the very least he wanted to keep the channel of communication open between them. Finally, he spoke. "It is good that you have told me of this."

"Are you sure?" she asked timidly. "The gods don't like it when I share too much. It makes them nervous."

"That will never be the case with me, dear one. I want you to tell me everything."

"Everything?"

"Absolutely. But first, there is something I need to attend to. Will you meet me later?"

"Yes."

"Good. I'll come find you this afternoon. Until then you'll keep this between us?"

Nephthys nodded. "I will."

Seth beamed at her, and in his smile Nephthys saw a glimpse of what they could be together. The timing was wrong, she knew, but she also knew of his unhappiness. By telling him what she'd learned, she wanted to offer him something to look forward to and to focus on. If she was successful, she might be able to sway him toward the path she hoped he'd take.

As Nephthys walked away, the stars whispered that she had no control over Seth's choices and that he'd do what he was going to do anyway. She could only wish he wouldn't. If he could just see the things she could . . . but none of them did. Not even Isis, her beloved sister.

Nephthys hummed to herself as she made her way through the halls toward Amun-Ra. He was as hardheaded as Seth, and it was a challenge to rouse him to speak of anything other than duty. His dreams were locked away so tightly that no one, not even she, as soft-spoken and perceptive as she was, could bring them to the surface. It didn't stop her from trying, though. He felt so alone in his responsibilities, and she knew her presence offered him peace and a pleasant distraction.

She signaled a servant to bring tea and settled in the chair where they met each morning. Amun-Ra nodded as he entered and she smiled, her lips hidden behind her steaming teacup as he took the seat next to her. The stars whispered again, but she knew there was no manipulating Amun-Ra. Unlike Seth, there was no swaying him toward one course or another. He'd need to come to the decision on his own and in the time that felt right to him. Nephthys sighed. The wait would be long and tiresome, but it would be worth it. She had to believe that.

While Nephthys and Amun-Ra talked of godly things as they sipped tea and sat in pools of sunshine streaming in through the latticed windows of Amun-Ra's palace, Isis stood in the darkened stables peering at the curious animal that chewed oats lazily as it watched her. She was sure that the strange creature must be the reason Osiris had called her to the stables, and she let out an irritated breath.

It wasn't going to work. He was likely hoping to distract her again. He'd done it often over the centuries she'd known him. When she was cross with him over one thing or another, he'd bring her a flower she'd never seen, or a fluffy rabbit or kitten. Soon she'd forget all the reasons she'd been upset and pepper him with questions about his adventures.

She had no idea what this animal was called or where he might have found it, but she had to admit it was interesting. In appearance its face resembled a dog or a jackal but with long, tufted, square-tipped ears that stood straight up. Its legs were also long and lean like that of a gazelle, but this creature was no dog.

In mannerism, it was more like a horse. It was gentle and was putting away oats faster than any animal she'd ever seen. "I guess you're hungry," she said with a laugh as she stretched out a hand. Isis touched the creature's long neck and it moved closer, enjoying her caress. When she began scratching, it made a mewling sort of whine and angled its head so she could reach the best spots.

Long-lashed brown eyes blinked as it turned, wagging its bushy tail to sink its head back in the bucket of oats for another mouthful. At the same time, it angled its body so Isis could continue scratching. She obliged the animal with a fond pat. "You're a sweet thing, aren't you?"

"I like to think so," a voice behind her said.

Isis twirled around. "Seth. What are you doing here?" Isis asked.

"Looking for you," he said with a grin that looked a touch too intense.

"I'm waiting for Osiris, but you can stay until he arrives," she offered.

The grin slipped from Seth's face. "As you wish." He inclined his head, and as he did so, he waved his fingers and unmade a rather significant section of Osiris's garden, one that would be sorely missed by the god of weeds. Perhaps it would distract Osiris long enough to give him a chance to talk with Isis.

Stepping forward, he leaned over the stall where she watched the animal and wrinkled his nose at the smell. He'd rather take her to a different location, but he knew Isis wouldn't leave, not when Mr. Too-Handsome-for-His-Own-Good was on his way. Perhaps, though, if he revealed his secret, she'd be shocked enough to agree to a demonstration elsewhere after he confessed.

"Isn't it beautiful?" Isis said, pointing to the animal.

Seth could see nothing remarkable in the creature. In fact, as far as he could tell, it served no purpose. It was too small to ride upon. It didn't seem intelligent enough or soft enough to be a pet. It ate grain, which meant it needed to be fed. And as an herbivore, it was essentially useless in keeping the rodent population in check.

"Lovely," he said drily, no longer looking at the creature. "Isis?" he began.

"Yes?"

"I wanted to speak with you." Seth's mouth suddenly went dry and, for the life of him, he couldn't remember a single rehearsed line. Not when the lovely goddess trained her stormy eyes upon him.

"Go on," she encouraged, standing up. Her body stiffened, as if bracing itself for what would come next.

Seth stood too, bristling at having to look up at her. He wasn't short, at least not when compared with mortals, but Isis stood several inches above him. When he took her as a bride he'd make sure to set her throne lower than his. It would not do to have a wife who commanded more attention than he did. "I . . . I wanted to tell you that I've come into my power." He hadn't meant to state it so bluntly or with the awkward lack of confidence in his voice, but it was the best he seemed able to do. He was slightly mollified when Isis's face lit with enthusiasm.

"Really? That is wonderful!"

"It is." He grinned a bit sheepishly. "I wanted you

to be the first to hear about it."

"I'm honored. So?" Isis clasped his hand. "What is it?"

"It's . . . well . . ." Seth cast his eyes about the stables, looking for something unimportant. He found a small milking stool and set it between them. "Just watch. It's better if I show you."

Seth raised his hand and the stool shimmered and then disappeared. Truthfully, it was painfully easy to unmake an inanimate object. He gleaned no additional power from doing such a thing, so he considered it a waste of his energy. Whatever life force the wood of the stool had at one time had long since vanished. Still, it impressed Isis. She clapped her hands.

"That's amazing!" She spun around. "Where did it go? Can you move anything?" she asked. "What about people?"

"I didn't move the stool," Seth said, slightly uneasy. "I . . . unmade it."

"Unmade? What does that mean?"

"It means it has now ceased to exist."

"So you destroyed it?"

Seth shook his head. "To destroy is to break

something apart. In a case like that, the matter still exists. I erased the thing from the cosmos. And the answer to your former question is yes, I can do it to anything."

"But what happens when—"

He lifted a hand with a flourish. "Like I said, they cease to exist. If it's a living thing like a tree or an animal, part of its life essence is transferred to me and the rest of it returns to the Waters of Chaos."

"The Waters of . . . Are you sure?"

"Very sure. I've traveled there myself and tested it."

"But that means you've killed—"

Seth interrupted, holding up a finger. "Unmade."

Isis fluttered her wings and there was a telltale crease in her forehead that meant she was displeased with him. "Killed, unmade, what's the difference?" she questioned.

Seth frowned. This conversation wasn't headed in the direction he wanted. "I think you're missing the bigger picture."

"And what picture is that?" Isis asked.

"The Waters of Chaos are being refilled." He took hold of her shoulder and gritted his teeth when she flinched. "Re*filled,* Isis. Do you know what that means?"

He paused and was rewarded with the widening of her eyes. "It means more beings can be created," she answered soberly.

"Yes!" He nodded with overflowing enthusiasm.

The possibilities surged through Isis's mind. With the Waters of Chaos refilled, she could have a child. Maybe even more than one. She could be a mother.

"Can you fill the Waters by unmaking things without life?" she asked. "Items like the stool?"

"No. Only unmaking the living adds to the Waters. The more potent the life, the more the Waters rise."

"But to destroy the living is wrong," she said.

He sighed impatiently. "Not destroy. Unmake. But don't you see? You can help me."

"Help you? How so?"

"Help me choose what to unmake. With you by my side we'll be in perfect balance. Opposites but equals, my chaos and your creation. Your wisdom and goodness will keep me in check. I will be the fiery god of vengeance while you will be my icy counterpart—the goddess who banks the flames and offers relief and healing."

When she just stared at him, her eyes full of doubt and questions, he pressed, "Isis, I know you dislike the rules as much as I do. Think about what we could do. Together. I can give you what you long for. The mortals and creations you decide to save, I will pass over. Those you love can live for eternity. Surely that's worth the price of a few trees and flowers." He deliberately misled her. It would take much more than trees and flowers to make someone immortal, especially if he was absorbing a share of their life energy. But she wasn't ready to know that. Not yet.

Isis sucked in a breath, struck by an idea. She could save Baniti. It could be done. If she took Seth's side, he would allow her to do it.

"What is it you want from me, exactly?" Isis asked.

Seth cocked his head and gave her a small sneer. She was coming around to his way of seeing things. He knew it. Watching her had paid off. She was his. Not even the great Isis could deny his power.

"I want *you,*" he stated simply.

"Me?"

"Yes. Is it really so shocking? You are a beautiful

woman. Not only that, but you have the gift of spells and healing. My wish is that we join ourselves together, create a bond between us."

"But bonds between the gods are forbidden. Besides, even if they were not, I do not love you."

Seth shrugged as if it was of no concern to him, but in truth he seethed at the idea of her entertaining feelings for someone else. "We will change the rules. And . . . love will come in time," he said.

"And if it does not?"

He turned away from Isis, not wanting her to see how her words angered him. "If it does not, we will deal with it together, privately," he said out loud, while inwardly, he wondered at the possibility of unmaking a person's feelings. Would it damage the mind or the heart? It would be a risk to attempt such a thing on his bride. He'd test it out on others before working his power on her. He'd need her mind to be fully intact so she could write spells.

When Seth stepped away, Isis gripped the rail of the enclosure. She stared at the animal, which came up and rubbed its head against her hand. It was out of oats and was likely nudging her for more. Absentmindedly, she stroked it as she considered Seth's proposal. The ability to save Baniti and to have her own children was the dearest wish of her heart. But could she sacrifice other creations so that they would live? It came back to Amun-Ra's answer from before. Who or what would give up their lives to save the ones she loved?

Then there was the fact that Seth wanted her in the way a man desires a woman. Osiris had been right about that. *Osiris.* Isis couldn't deny that she'd given great thought to binding herself to another god, despite the edict that forbade it, but she'd never thought it would be with Seth.

Could she walk away from her feelings for Osiris and dedicate herself to Seth? She felt no love for him. Isis had no desire to be near him. She never missed him when he was gone. Truthfully, she rarely gave him any thought when he wasn't in her presence.

But when Osiris was not at her side, she ached for him. She wanted to be held by him. Longed to be kissed by him again the way he had kissed her the night before. Isis couldn't imagine an eternity without him.

A cold thought entered her heart: if Seth found out, would he unmake Osiris so that her love would have no other outlet? She could not allow such a thing to happen. As much as she wanted a child, as important as saving Baniti was, she knew that what Seth proposed was wrong.

Isis turned to Seth and gave him a pitying sort of sisterly smirk.

His whole body tightened in response. Seth knew what her answer would be before she even spoke.

"Seth, I want you to know that I've given your offer serious thought," she began, "but I'm afraid —"

Seth seized her arm. Any softness in his face had been replaced with steel. *How dare she pity him?* "Do *not* think to refuse me, Isis," he hissed. "I know this will come as a surprise, but I'll give you some time to consider my proposal. And be warned, it is my desire that you belong to me, body and soul. I will accept nothing less. I *deserve* nothing less," he spat. "And just so you understand the nature of my power . . ."

Wrenching her toward the wooden rail, Seth forced her to watch as he unmade the creature she'd become so recently enamored with. "No. Please!" she cried, and stretched out her hand just as it disappeared.

When she collapsed in a heap at his feet, sobbing,

a surge of pleasure ran through him. Seth crouched down next to her and lifted a fingertip to her wet cheek. He rubbed a tear between his fingers and the corner of his mouth lifted. He enjoyed seeing the glorious goddess reduced to a weeping supplicant.

"Perhaps you need just a bit more convincing," he said. Closing his eyes, he stretched his power further than he ever had before, testing the boundaries of his ability and unmade every single one of the strange little creatures that Isis adored. They winked out of existence in every dark corner of the cosmos.

Then something interesting happened. The life energy of hundreds of thousands of creatures entered his being at once. The feeling was so overwhelming, so utterly shocking, that he couldn't absorb it immediately. In his mind the screams of countless innocent creatures railed upon him as he stole their life essence. His head throbbed worse than it ever had before.

The unmaking he'd done in the past had been disturbing, but the suffering was usually so brief he could easily ignore the twinge of guilt that came with it. This time he had to look at what he'd done with an all-seeing eye, and what he saw made him tremble. He clutched his hair and pulled.

Then, though it felt like an eternity, the pangs of death passed through him. The pain subsided, and he realized the effects had lasted just a few seconds. When it was gone, the power of all the lives he'd ripped away filled him, effectively snuffing out the waves of guilt that threatened to bring him to his knees. The raw power was unlike anything he'd ever felt before.

Seth was stronger. Bigger. His eyesight had improved a hundredfold. And he was hungry. His body shook with new energy, and then he began to transform. One moment he was himself, and the next his body had become one of the very creatures he'd blinked out of existence.

The effect was disturbing, but it was also very, very interesting. After a terrifying moment where he was trapped in the body of the creature he'd unmade, wondering if it was the cosmic punishment for his actions, he shifted back into his normal state. It had happened so quickly that Isis hadn't even noticed.

Her wings had curled around her body, shielding herself from his view. Seth flexed his fingers and ran a hand over his ears. In his mind he could still sense the long ears of the creature and feel the air as it passed over the sensitive hairs on the insides of them. He imagined the stench of the creature still permeating his skin, and he longed to immerse his body in a warm pool and scrub the memory of it from his flesh.

But almost immediately he wondered if he could transform into the creature again. If he retained such an ability because he'd made the animal extinct, could he not do it again, with a different species? Impatient to practice this newfound power and make a list of potential animals to test, Seth rose.

"What have you done?" Isis whispered from the shadow of her wings, still fixating on the one animal when so much more had happened in such a short period of time. When Seth didn't immediately answer, Isis lifted her tearstained face to look at him, praying he hadn't done something horrible to Osiris or her sister.

"Oh, that." Seth had long since moved on and was ready to quit the tiresome conversation. "I've unmade every single one of those creatures. You'll never come across one again. They're now extinct."

Isis's mouth dropped open in silent shock. Her body shuddered. Her wings quivered and Seth lifted an eyebrow, wondering if this was the moment she'd fight back. But then her jaw trembled and she tucked her head beneath her wings again. What a delight to twist the emotions of the great goddess Isis beneath his thumb.

Seth boldly took hold of one of her soft wings and tugged, brutally exposing her face. "I'll leave you alone now to ponder your choices, Isis. See that you make the right decision. I expect you'll come to it eventually."

Taking his leave of the stables, Seth crossed the barrier to the mortal realm, looking for the next animal species he could experiment on. Perhaps the next time he saw Isis, he'd be able to transform at will into a great cat or a bear or even a dragon. Imagining the myriad of ways he could torture Osiris and tame Isis to his will brought a delighted sneer to his face.

Osiris found the weeping goddess a short time later. "Isis?" He knelt next to her. "Are you all right? What has happened?"

"It's Seth." Isis reached out and took hold of Osiris's arm as she told him what had happened. Uncharacteristic rage filled the gentle-natured god. When she told Osiris that Seth had destroyed not only the sweet creature but every one of them that existed in the cosmos,

Osiris's hands shook. To stop them, he drew Isis up and into his arms.

"It was called a typhon," Osiris murmured as he stroked her hair.

"And now they no longer exist," Isis said. "You were right," she admitted, blinking the tears from her eyes. "He desires me. Seth thinks he can rip my heart from my chest and keep it for his own just as he ripped his way out of his mother's womb."

Osiris cupped her face in his hands. "He cannot take what you do not offer."

"His power is great and terrible," Isis said. "You didn't see it. And I worry that he—"

"What is it?" he asked as she stepped away from him.

Wanting to comfort her but not knowing how, he simply moved closer. She shifted her wing behind her, wrapping her arms around his waist, and laid her head on his shoulder. "I fear that he will try to unmake you."

Stiffening, Osiris asked, "Do you think he can do such a thing? Unmake a god?"

"I don't know. I only know that the possibility exists and that he intends to take me as his own. If he threatens to harm those I love, I'll have no choice but to accept his terms."

"You will not!" Osiris stated abruptly, and when Isis's eyes shot to his, he tried to calm himself. "You will not," he said more gently. "I will not allow him to force you into such an arrangement. We'll go to Amun-Ra."

"No." She shook her head and stepped out of his embrace. "You know Amun-Ra. He'd come up with a wait-and-see strategy. Either that or he'll just add more rules to his long list. Even if Amun-Ra wanted to do something about Seth, he might not be able to. Meanwhile, while we rest on our laurels, Seth will harm living creatures—plants, animals, even mortals. Do you want him to destroy your great rain forests? Your fields and your orchards?"

Osiris sobered. "That must have been what happened to the nut trees."

"You mean the place we were together last night?" A chill shot ice through her veins. *Had Seth been watching them?*

Osiris nodded. "It suddenly disappeared. Nothing in the entire area is growing. There isn't a weed, a nut, or a worm to be seen in the whole place. What's more, the ground is now infertile. Barren. Nothing will ever grow there again. Such power . . . it's . . . it's unimaginable. We've got to find a way to stop him."

"We do," Isis agreed. "I won't have him erase the people I love from existence." The goddess bit her lip and then sucked in a breath, turning to Osiris. "Why did you summon me?"

"What?"

"Why did you summon me here? Was it to show me the animal, the typhon?"

"Yes," he answered automatically. Then seeing her crestfallen expression, he clapped a hand on the back of his neck and rubbed. "No."

Her eyes lifted. "Why, then? Tell me, Osiris."

"I . . . I did want to show you the animal, but it was just an excuse to get you to talk to me." He glanced at her face but couldn't read the thoughts behind her stormy eyes.

"What did you want to talk about?" she asked pointedly.

"Us." He sighed.

"Us?"

Osiris settled his hands on her shoulders. The

sparkle of a forgotten tear lingered on her sooty eyelash. He hoped he would never be the cause of her tears. Not ever again. Steeling himself, Osiris said, "You've shared your feelings openly with me and I haven't been as forthcoming. But now I see that it would be wrong for me to deny you from knowing mine."

She sucked in a breath. "Then tell me, Osiris. How do you feel?"

The way she looked at him was intoxicating. She was the perfect mix of power and vulnerability. He found he couldn't resist touching her and cupped her cheek, brushing his thumb over the still shiny trails of her tears. "I told you I needed to think, and I did. All night. When you told me of your feelings before, it shook me. I'd never considered such a thing. But even as I tried to set thoughts of you aside, I found I couldn't. Your face haunted me. And last night, when we kissed . . ."

Isis shifted closer and Osiris took hold of her hands and brought them to his chest. "Yes?" she encouraged.

"Last night I realized that in denying my feelings for you, I was denying myself happiness."

"Then are you saying—?"

He pressed her hands flat against his chest. "I'm saying that I love you, Isis. That my heart beats for no one but you."

Isis found it difficult to breathe for a moment. Osiris stood before her declaring himself, and she couldn't bring a single word to mind in response to his declaration.

He squeezed her hands. "Isis? Did you hear me?"

"Yes," she whispered.

"So . . . that's it? You have nothing to say?" Osiris asked a bit nervously.

She grinned. That she could make the handsome god uneasy gave her a tiny boost of joy. Isis slid her arms up around his neck and touched her lips to his in a brief kiss, delighting in the small shudder that ran through his body. "I love you, too," she murmured against his mouth.

Isis felt his smile but was soon lost in his passionate embrace. Each touch was a new discovery; each kiss she committed to memory. When his hands stroked the sensitive feathers on the insides of her wings, her body trembled with pleasure. She had longed to be held by this man. Now that she was finally in his arms, Isis recognized that her imagination had been sorely limited.

Being able to express her love for Osiris and feel

his love in return with every touch of his hand, every kiss, and the tender way he gazed upon her was a magic all its own. This was what she'd always desired—someone who would hold her heart as she held his. This fragile, new, and glorious thing they had discovered together was so precious to her, so perfect, that there was only one thing that could mar it—Seth.

Pressing lightly against his chest, Isis broke the kiss. "Do you pledge your love to me and only me, then?" Isis asked.

Her expression was intense, the colors in her eyes churning. It pained Osiris that she could still doubt him. "Yes," he answered softly. "Whatever the consequences may be, and for as long as the cosmos allows our love to exist, I am yours, Isis, as you are mine."

Isis took his face in her hands. "Then, Osiris, let us make an unbreakable vow."

CHAPTER 5

HUSBANDRY

"An unbreakable vow?" he echoed.

"Yes. I've given the idea a great amount of thought." Taking his hands, Isis pulled Osiris deeper into the stables and cast a spell to make sure they were truly alone. When she was satisfied, she explained, "You know that Amun-Ra sent Shu to separate Geb and Nut?"

Osiris nodded. "She was his secret wife, but the stars exposed their relationship and Amun-Ra used the god of the wind to keep them apart."

"I will not have such a thing happen to us."

"How would we stop it?" he asked. "The stars are everywhere."

"That's not exactly true. There is a rift in the

heavens when the night succumbs to the day. If you stand in just the right spot, the stars are blind."

"Where? And why have I never heard of this?"

"It is at the pinnacle of Mount Babel. I heard of it from my sister. Nephthys told me it is the only place she finds peace from her visions."

"But Babel is a forbidden place. The gods aren't supposed to go there. It is an area of great confusion and contradiction. The harmony of the cosmos is fragmented in that location. How has she managed to remain sane?"

Isis frowned. "She might not be. At least, not fully. Nephthys has been affected by it, I believe, but she suffers for her visions more than she shows, and I wouldn't take away a thing that gives her comfort. I certainly wouldn't betray her to Amun-Ra. Besides, I have been able to heal her mind when she returns. Mostly." Isis shook off thoughts of her sister and focused again on their own problem. "Babel comes with its dangers, certainly, but that is exactly why it suits our purposes."

Osiris touched her face. "I'll not lose you to the mountain's madness," he said softly.

"You won't. Even if we are lost, we will find one another."

"How can you be certain?"

Isis waved her hand and two small vases appeared. One was a blue glazed faience with a silver feline head for a lid, and the second was carved alabaster with a golden cobra on top. Carefully, Isis removed the lids of the jars and circled her arms over them, murmuring a spell as she did so. "We will each hold a piece of the other's heart. They will guide our steps until we find one another."

She placed her hand over her heart and closed her eyes. When she drew it back, a lovely amethyst heart scarab sat in her palm with wings made of gold pounded so thin they were almost transparent. She held it out to Osiris, who took it. He marveled at the luminous gem and traced his fingers lightly over its facets.

As he did, he could feel the beat of her heart. It both soothed and frightened him. The idea that he could lose her—and what's more, lose himself—scared him to the depths of his being. But more than anything, he wanted to prove himself worthy of her love and trust. The least he could do was trust her in return.

With great care, Osiris placed her heart scarab in the alabaster vase and closed the lid. Then he murmured a spell of his own to seal it with the sap from a tree that was so sticky, he'd never found a thing in nature to dissolve it. When he was satisfied, he called forth his own heart scarab—a gleaming, golden diamond framed with shafts of ripened wheat stalks the color of sunshine instead of wings.

"It's beautiful," she said as he handed it to her.

It was such a strange sensation to have your heart seized by another. *Besieged* would be a better word, for Isis had surrounded him. Captured him, body and soul. As he stood there in the shadow of her wings, he perceived that he was her willing prisoner, he'd offered up his wrists to shackle himself, and yet he knew there was no place in the cosmos that could offer him such contentment.

What they were doing was mad, impulsive. But wasn't love a form of madness? For a fraction of a second, he wondered if perhaps the love he felt was a spell she'd cast upon him that caused him to leap where he would normally be cautious. Then he cast aside the notion. He was still the master of his own desires. Besides, even if Isis had bewitched him, he no longer cared.

He'd seen the sickness of love in others before, but Osiris hadn't understood it then, not fully. Now he recognized the condition in himself. Isis was an intoxicating flower and he was a helpless bee mesmerized by her. Now that he'd tasted her, he was dusted. Filled with her honeyed pollen. If the weight of it dragged him down so he drowned in her embrace, then he'd consider his life well spent.

Isis was his purpose.

Isis was his everything.

All his life he'd been looking for her, and he hadn't known it.

Osiris watched Isis put his heart scarab into her own blue vase and seal it shut before turning to him. "We'll need to be careful with Seth," she said, pulling him from his thoughts. Isis walked away a few paces and then turned back. "It is nearly time for the swelling of the Nile. Am I correct?"

"Yes. I oversee its rising so that the crops will grow. It's still a little early, but the time is at hand."

"Then this is what you will do. Go there today and raise the Nile, even if it is a bit early. Water unmakes and then makes anew. I will be able to channel this power into my spell. Besides, it will be a good omen."

When Osiris agreed that this could be

accomplished, she continued, "When the sun sinks below the horizon, make your way to Mount Babel. Keep my heart with you at all times. I will use the hours ahead to traverse the skies, sweep our deeds into hidden corners, and prepare my spell. After the sun sets, I will go to Babel and seek you out. When we find one another on the mountain, we will hide in the dark shadows until the space between the night and the dawn, and after that nothing will be able to keep us apart."

Isis knew she was asking much of him, and yet there was no other way for the two of them to be together. In truth, she wasn't sure if she could channel the power she'd need to cast such a potent spell. If he wavered in any way it wouldn't work and she'd lose him in more ways than one. "Are you sure this is what you want, Osiris? Once we are bound, nothing can come between us. Even death. It is a weighty thing I ask of you. If you have doubts . . ."

Osiris slid his hand up her neck and dipped down to kiss her lush lips, stopping her midsentence and hoping he was conveying the depth of his emotion in his embrace. He pulled her against his body and when she softened into him, the tension finally leaving her shoulders, he murmured, "I will take my leave of you now as we have planned, but until I see you again, know that this kiss is my secret vow. Let Seth move against us. Let the stars try to thwart us. Let Amun-Ra forbid us. We will unite by the force of our wills and the force of our desire, and slake our solitary souls in the light of our love for one another."

"And if I fail?" she asked softly.

"It won't matter," Osiris answered as he stroked her hair. "Tonight my heart will be pierced with either terrible joy or terrific sorrow. Either way, it belongs to you." With that, Osiris kissed her, his lips sealing his fervent promise.

Isis raised her wings, enveloping both of them inside their span. They held on to one another desperately, both of them knowing the risk they were taking. And then, after a last searing kiss, they reluctantly parted. Osiris watched Isis leave first, her blue vase with his heart scarab inside tucked under her arm.

"Be safe, my beloved," he whispered as his eyes traced her path across the sky. When she was gone, he took up the alabaster vase and placed it in the satchel he always traveled with. Then Osiris raised his arms and sank below the ground, passing through the dark divide between the realm of the gods and the Earth.

The long hours of the day passed slowly for Osiris, and his thoughts often drifted to Isis and the spell she would weave. They were both risking much. Perhaps Amun-Ra would take away their abilities after he discovered what they'd done. Maybe he'd banish them to the Earth and make them eke out a life as mortals. The idea didn't bother him as much as it perhaps should have.

With his knowledge of agriculture and hers as a healer, they could live a very fine life together, even if it was only in the time span of a mortal. He rubbed his jaw and adjusted his pack as he strode forward through the city, heading toward the farmland and the green growth rising along the borders of the Nile.

Isis might regret the loss of her wings if she became mortal. If he was honest with himself, he would regret the loss of her wings, too. They were glorious to behold, and the feel of them was a sensory experience he couldn't begin to describe. But the wings, though a part of her, weren't the whole of her.

He'd still have the woman even if she wasn't a goddess. And a woman such as Isis was all a man could ask for. Even as mortals they'd be happy. Osiris stopped in his tracks as he suddenly realized that with mortality there was the possibility of more than just being with the woman he loved.

Osiris had never considered having children. But now the idea took root in his mind. A son? A daughter? A whole houseful of children? He thought of all the things he'd learned as a god. All the things he could share with and teach his offspring. His heart raced as he realized how badly he wanted a family.

Just as he hadn't acknowledged his desire for Isis until she proposed the idea of a relationship, he'd never allowed himself to ponder the idea of fatherhood. Isis had been right. Vulnerability, in this case being stripped of powers and becoming mortal, was freeing.

Every instinct inside him said there was more. That he could do more, be more, than what he was. Was it wrong for him to reach for it? Maybe. But he'd reach anyway. He wasn't worried about the consequences. If the worst thing that could happen was staying with Isis as a mortal, Osiris thought he could live with that.

Having reached the Nile, Osiris raised his arms and recited the spell that would cause the river to swell and flood out of its bed. He couldn't help welcoming the smile that lifted his cheeks as he looked up at the sun. When the muddy water reached his feet and lapped at his ankles, he laughed and happily thought of his own overreaching. Whether the path he trod with Isis hurled him up among celestial realms or led him to toiling in the muck of mortality, it didn't matter as long as they were together.

The water of the Nile kissed the parched soil. When it dried, the rich slurry it left behind would nourish the crops that grew on the riverbanks. Thousands would be fed. It wasn't a little thing, the swelling of the Nile. The decaying things the river carried would bring new life. It was a completely natural process. He might have to take away a part of himself to be with Isis, but by doing so, he'd nourish the new thing developing between them.

Amun-Ra had always harangued them about sacrifice, Osiris thought as he waded through the water back toward the fields. He'd taught them that sometimes a thing needed to be lost before others could gain. Maybe if he explained his beliefs to Amun-Ra, the great god would understand. Then again, maybe not.

After shaking the mud from his sandaled feet, he walked through the fields at a mortal's pace. The grain was thick and golden and the air carried the sweet scent of warm hay baked in the morning sun. The day was beautiful, and he spent the hours thinking of his love and of the coming trials that they needed to hurdle so they could become one.

* * *

The hours passed quickly for Isis. She wrote her spell over and over again, mumbling it to herself and then scratching out the words, testing each term for potency. When Isis was satisfied, she ate heartily, knowing she'd need all her energy to enact the spell. She then flew toward the setting sun and let the light fill her frame. She gathered its might in her wings, and as the sun lit each feather, she felt healing warmth trickle into her veins.

Not even the gods knew her healing power rested in her feathers. If a feather was lost, a very rare occurrence that usually only happened when she slept, she searched her bedchamber until she found it. Even detached from her body, her feathers carried great power and, on occasion, she'd gifted one to a mortal who desperately needed it.

Baniti never knew that when Isis found her as a child that she was dying. Isis had gifted her a feather that was absorbed into the mortal's back. But even so, Isis had only been able to keep the sickness at bay for the span of her mortal life. She'd tried to channel all the power she possessed through every feather she had when she'd attempted to heal her, but the magic stayed within her and still she was unable to eradicate the sickness from Baniti's frail and aging body.

Now she hovered in the sky, absorbing every drop of sunshine she could so that she might enact the most difficult spell she'd ever created. Isis wished she could tell her sister, but anything Nephthys knew the stars knew, too. She couldn't risk it. Not until the thing was done.

When night fell, she flew to the dark mountain that marked the edge of Duat. Flying to the top would be the easiest path, but it was also the most dangerous one. Proximity to Mount Babel twisted the perceptions. She could easily crash into the mountain or veer off and plunge into the sea. Such a thing might not kill her, but it would raise an alarm in Heliopolis and that she could not have. The best way to reach the pinnacle was to climb and the climb would take hours.

Isis landed at the base of the mountain, clutching the vase that held Osiris's heart scarab, and sought out a path. At first, the ascent was easy, pleasant even. The smell of sap permeated the air and the crunch of pine needles beneath her feet kept her grounded even when the whispers began.

Nephthys had explained the whispers often enough that Isis understood, at least in theory, how it worked. The stars watched over everything, knew everything, but they only shared what was important. This did not mean what they shared was important to *an individual* but what was important from their perspective.

The whispers made more sense when dreaming, Nephthys had told her, but seeing things that would happen in the future was maddening in its own way. Isis didn't envy her sister's gift. Not at all. And being on the mountain made it even worse as the stars became confused. Until she reached the peak, which functioned as a giant adder stone, she would be at their mercy.

Nothing she heard or saw on the mountain could be trusted. The only thing she could be sure of was the heart she clutched in her hands. Through it she could tell that Osiris was also on the mountain, though she didn't know where. Not yet. The heart would beat faster when he was near. Regardless, the spell couldn't be performed until they were together at the pinnacle of the mountain, and only at the right time.

As she climbed, following deer trail switchbacks, the whispers became more insistent. They led her once to the hollow of a tree and told her to hide. Her mind insisted she was in danger so she did what the stars told her to. She shivered inside the tree trunk, her mind erupting with the visions the stars sent.

In her churning dreams, Isis saw herself sitting disconsolate in a tomb that smelled of mold and burning incense, fat teardrops dripping from her cheeks. She screamed at the sound of a double-bit axe cutting through something, though she didn't know what it was. Her sister was nearby but something was very wrong with her. The unimaginable had happened.

In another vision Isis saw herself married to Seth and watched as he overthrew all the gods. Because the Waters of Chaos were then filled with the life essence of her family, she was able to conceive and brought forth twins—a boy and a girl whom Seth named Dawn and Dusk. He proudly displayed them to his retinue of henchmen, those who served him wholly and completely. Each and every one bowed, and flattered, and fell at his feet as Seth crowed about his offspring and how they would draw the eyes of all who saw them.

When Isis looked upon her children, however, there was nothing behind her eyes, for she only saw those who had been destroyed so that her children might live. As badly as she craved motherhood, her unhappiness could not be overcome, for each sunset and sunrise was tinged with blood. She found nothing beautiful in them at all.

Wrenching herself out of the tree trunk, Isis tried to cast aside the terrible vision and willed herself to press on. As she trudged ahead, Amun-Ra's voice castigated her for her wrong choices and urged her to abandon her notions of saving Baniti. This was something that had already happened. At least, she had thought so. Now she couldn't be sure.

After hours of wandering, the heart in the jar leapt, meaning Osiris was even closer. Isis quickened her pace. She knew she'd lost too much time in the tree and hoped they weren't too late. If they could find each other, they could navigate the insanity of the mountain more easily.

Osiris was, in fact, much higher on the mountain than Isis. He'd been able to use his power over growing things to stabilize his mind, but now the swirling stars were too much even for the larger trees of the forest to help. As he climbed, Osiris heard a woman's voice telling him that Isis's affection for him would flicker and the flame of her love would extinguish and die. He didn't believe it. He couldn't. The stars had to be spreading falsehoods.

Bracing his arm on a thick tree branch, he panted as his mind was overtaken. He saw Isis in a vision, her skin as radiant as the glittering Nile at sunset, and he had to lift his hand to shield his eyes when she looked upon him. The beauty of her face was nothing compared to the beauty that radiated from inside her. It was like staring directly into the sun.

Osiris was dazzled and blinded by her. Isis was a being so powerful, so resplendent, he gasped in awe, and marveled that such a creature should desire one such as him. Then his eyes widened when he saw her kneel over a lifeless form and raise her wings around him. She was trying to revive the person, and he knew doing such a thing would kill her. "No!" he cried, his voice echoing over the mountain. "No, Isis, I forbid it!"

The stars spun the vision away and showed him a man—no, a god. He was straight and tall and he looked familiar, though Osiris knew he'd never seen him before. The god was cast into the desert, where he was plagued with all manner of hardships. He was stung by scorpions and attacked by wild beasts, and he suffered the bites of poisonous serpents. Osiris longed to go to his aid but something restrained him, and when he took a step forward, he stumbled and his legs shook as if he were a newborn colt.

His mind was spinning dizzily, and when it stopped, he stood in a new place, one he recognized. It was Earth. Stark pyramids rose from the sand. Three young men stood atop them. There they drew forth power, so much that he knew their bodies couldn't contain it. As energy rushed toward them from all parts of the cosmos, the pyramids acted as conduits, swallowing the light at their bases and channeling it up to the men who stood on the tops.

Then the men did something he'd never seen before. They summoned the light into themselves and it exploded from their outstretched arms, creating an impossible triangle in the night sky. Why they did this, he did not know. Who they were was a mystery to him. He'd never met these gods before, but he couldn't deny they held the power of the cosmos in their hands. Despite this ability, the three men staggered and fell dead, and he watched as Anubis guided them to the afterlife.

One of the disembodied looked at Osiris as if he, too, could see him in the vision. It startled Osiris, but he felt no malice from the watcher. The young man nodded at him and then turned to follow the others. He reached out his hand to touch the larger man's shoulder, but as he did, Osiris felt a hand on his own shoulder. It startled him from his vision and he spun around.

"Isis," he said, blowing out a breath in relief. "I was . . ."

"Lost in a dream?"

"Yes."

"Don't think of it now," she murmured. "We'll speak of it tomorrow."

"Tomorrow," he echoed with a nod. There *would* be a tomorrow for the two of them. There had to be. He took hold of her hand and together they managed to finish the climb without becoming lost. Being close to each other grounded them like the trees had done for him farther down. "Why couldn't we climb the mountain side by side?"

"The stars couldn't see us together. Not until we were high enough that the madness obscured us from their sight."

"But won't they suspect what we're doing here? Since we're both climbing Mount Babel on the same night?"

Isis shook her head. "Nephthys explained to me that the stars don't see things linearly. All they know is that I have climbed the mountain and you have climbed the mountain. To them this could have happened centuries apart. And now that we are close to the adder stone, our forms will be obscured. Besides, the stars are reactionary. They won't move against us until we have sealed our union. When it is a sure thing, they will respond."

Isis and Osiris struggled together until they neared the summit and crouched beneath the branches of a tree. Osiris could tell it was more than a thousand years old. He sat at the base of its trunk and pulled her onto his lap, holding her close and murmuring words of comfort as the visions tormented her.

Then she returned the favor, stroking his brow and kissing his temple to help him discern what was true from what was not. Though, with Isis in his arms, the dreamworld visions he saw in his mind and what was real occasionally overlapped in a pleasant way, but mostly the experience was a never-ending torment he wished he could escape.

Once he thought he saw a young man, a dreamer, watching him. When he turned to look, no one was there, though he still felt the dreamer's eyes on the back of his neck. When Isis said it was time, he breathed a sigh of relief. They both stood and took the final steps to the top.

The moment the two of them passed through the edge of the forest and onto the stony ridge at the peak of Mount Babel, their minds quieted. It was a stark contrast to the mental noise that had been plaguing them for hours. Isis half laughed, half sobbed at the relief, and she stumbled against him. The terrain was unnatural, the stones looked almost polished, and great monoliths of it jutted up into the sky. It was as if they stood on the crown atop a giant's head.

The black sky above them was dark and thin, like space, but not a single star shone. It was like standing in . . . nothingness. It was as if he no longer had form or substance, and gravity no longer held his feet in place. Osiris swayed dizzily and panted, the breath escaping him.

Then he became aware of the shivering woman in his arms, and when he looked upon her he felt centered and whole once more. He shook her. "Isis . . . Isis . . . look at me." She lifted her tearstained face to his and he wiped the offending drops away with his thumb. "We're here, beloved. Just focus on me."

Isis sucked in a few shaky breaths and nodded. "I knew this place would be different, but I never imagined . . ." Her voice dropped off as she thought of her sister and how unbearable her life must be. Osiris squeezed her hands and she looked up at his earnest face. "Are you ready?" she asked.

"I am."

Her heart swelled at the trust and the love she saw. "Close your eyes," Isis said, and when he did, she cast a small spell. It was one of cleansing and preparation for what was to come. Warmth trickled from the roots of her hair down her body to her fingertips and toes. When it was done, she asked him to open his eyes.

When Osiris did, he saw that they were both renewed, as if they'd bathed in a golden waterfall. Isis was breathtaking in a gossamer dress spun of stars and moonlight. Her wings were tucked at her back and her hair cascaded in thick waves that ended at her waist. "You look beautiful," he said warmly.

"As do you."

He hadn't noticed his own clothes. He looked down and saw he wore a tunic and breeches of sparkling white as well. Both of them had bare feet, and he realized with a start that the giant adder stone they stood upon thrummed with an energy that he could feel in his soles. "What next?" he asked.

"We must be quick," Isis said. "The time between the night and the day is short. Take my heart in your hand as I take yours." Osiris broke the jar holding Isis's heart and brushed aside the shattered pieces of pottery until he spied the amethyst heart scarab. When each of them was ready, she said, "This is a threshing. The best within each of us will rise up, weave together, and become something new. Something that cannot be unraveled."

She looked into his eyes as if asking again if this was what he truly desired. Osiris nodded assuredly, giving her an encouraging smile, and Isis began to chant. It was a complex spell that spoke of secret wishes, bindings, and the sharing of hearts. Then she called forth the power of a true syzygy. He'd never heard of such a thing being used in a spell before.

A syzygy was a common-enough celestial occurrence. It happened when three celestial bodies in the same gravitational system, such as the Earth, the moon, and the sun, aligned. But Isis spoke of a true syzygy. This had never happened before. At least, not in the time he'd been alive.

A true syzygy still involved three celestial bodies, but the alignment was of a permanent nature. Once the alignment transpired, the three would be locked together, never to move again. If Isis could call forth the power of a true syzygy, then her spells could indeed rival Seth's abilities. Now the vision he'd seen of Isis made more sense. Her entire body was filled with light.

As she concluded her spell, Isis smiled and Osiris thought she'd never looked so lovely or radiant. "Is it done, then?" he asked.

"Almost. There is just one more piece and then we will be yoked together eternally, bound in such a way that not even the stars will be able to separate us."

"What must I do?" Osiris asked softly.

"You must take my heart into your own and then I will tell you my secret name."

"You will do this, too?" he asked.

She nodded, her eyes bright. What she was asking him harnessed the most primal magic. To know someone's true name was to have complete power over them. It required an unflinching level of trust in another person and was unlike any other commitment in the heavens or beneath it. Any dereliction of honor, any breach of loyalty, even a tiny moment of waning courage or selfishness would cause great suffering for both of them. After they did this, the two of them would be able to see into one another's hearts and understand each other wholly, both the good and the bad.

Osiris didn't hesitate. He cupped her heart in his hand and placed it over his chest. Amethyst light burst from the gemstone as it sank into his frame and disappeared, its wings fluttering slightly as it burrowed into him and settled next to his own heart. Isis repeated the process with the golden scarab. As it eased into its new position, Isis caught the rich scents of the forest and of distant fields of grain.

Isis reached out her hands and Osiris took them, drawing her close. Just as the dark sky began to lighten they whispered their secret names to one another and the world tilted on its axis.

They were one.

They were unbreakable.

They were yoked in a bond that would last for eternity.

In the circle of each other's arms they stood for minutes or hours or millennia. They didn't know how long they remained rooted in place, gazes fixed upon one another. They didn't care, for in the shadows of Isis's wings all was still and silent.

Then Osiris kissed her and the world around them exploded.

CHAPTER 6

THRESHING

All at once, the great star of the sky, the all-seeing sun, cast its light over the mountain, and the impact of what they'd done was immediately felt. The mountaintop shook as Geb trembled in fear, causing an earthquake that almost broke apart the towering monoliths of the immense adder stone they stood upon.

The whispering of the stars became shouts. And the goddess Nut gathered the skirts of her clouds and drew them to her face, veiling herself as her giant teardrops fell upon all of Duat. Enormous tree limbs shifted their branches and hid in the shadows of one another, as if ashamed to have been caught shielding the couple.

From where they stood, clutching one another and gazing up into the heavens, Isis and Osiris could see the alteration they'd caused in the celestial law written among the stars. The shining orbs above, hidden by the light of the sun from all but the gods themselves, shifted and reorganized themselves, forming new constellations and groupings to allow for the spell Isis had wrought.

Both of them heard the summons that pealed through the sky like the call of a shrieking raptor. It was the time for reckoning, for Amun-Ra knew what had come to pass. Osiris squeezed his new wife's hand. "We must go."

Clutching her fingers, he turned to leave but paused when she drew back and pulled away. "They are distraught," she said, referring to the stars.

"We knew they would be."

The two of them looked up as the stars realigned. Some stars were extinguished while new stars ignited, bursting into glorious existence, their light burning bright as if to announce to anyone who glanced heavenward what Isis and Osiris had done.

Isis turned her gaze to her new husband and was troubled to see the worry on his face. "Do you regret it?"

she asked, slightly afraid of his response.

Osiris touched his forehead to hers. "No, Little One. My only regret is that we must now face our elders instead of celebrating the vows we have made this night."

Isis nodded, relieved at his answer, and all the love she felt for her him showed in the softness of her smile.

When Osiris started to make his way down the mountain, Isis took hold of his hand. "We are one now. Come. Fly with me."

Isis stretched out her wings and placed her hand on his heart. "Feel the strength of my wings in the heart scarab you carry," she said, and then, with a powerful thrust, Isis rose into the air.

Closing his eyes, Osiris sought out the second heart that beat within, the small amethyst that belonged to the one he had claimed, and embraced the surge of power he found there. The golden wings stirred in his chest. When he opened his eyes, to his delight, he was airborne, floating high above the mountain where Isis waited for him.

"Just think of me," she called out across the expanse of sky, "and your heart will bring you to mine."

The connection between them was amazing. It was unlike anything Osiris had ever felt before. Not only did he share in her power, he could now read her thoughts. Isis was hesitant to confront Amun-Ra, but she was not ashamed of their union. In fact, she was proud to belong to him. That she'd been able to accomplish a spell of such magnitude was startling, and yet it pleased her. A part of Isis longed to cast other spells that she'd been too apprehensive to attempt in the past.

As he explored her thoughts further, he realized just how dangerous a union such as theirs had been. She hadn't shared everything with him. If it hadn't worked, both of them would have been destroyed. If he had known this risk to her, he might have, at the very least, paused to consider the costs. Osiris didn't care about the risks to himself, and he found he held no animosity that she'd kept silent. Ultimately, he still would have gone through with it.

Isis chided him through his thoughts. *My love,* she whispered. *You are thinking too much. Try to let yourself enjoy the flight.*

Amazed at discovering the newfound ability to speak to her without a voice, Osiris sent her a myriad of thoughts: his gentle censure over her keeping the danger of the spell hidden from him, the wonder of feeling her emotions, the longing to hold her close and whisk her away to a hidden garden he'd never shared with anyone before, and, at last, his gratitude that she'd been patient enough to wait for him to come to her.

He drew closer to her and looked up just as she looked down. The smile she gave him was full of promises and secrets that just the two of them would share. *I wasn't that patient,* she said, and he could tell that his thoughts had pleased her. That was good. It would help to distract her from the unpleasantness waiting for them in Heliopolis.

Unfortunately, the unpleasantness took form quickly as Seth stormed into the council chamber not a minute after they'd arrived. Amun-Ra, whose lips had been pressed into a thin line when they'd entered, hadn't even spoken yet. He'd just stared at them. Nephthys stood at his side, and Isis noticed the forgotten tea setting for two on the side table. She raised an eyebrow and wondered why her sister might be having tea with Amun-Ra.

The first words out of Amun-Ra's mouth were

directed to Seth. "You were not summoned," he said simply.

"Are you going to try to diminish and excuse what they've done?" Seth immediately countered. "We've all seen the stars. They've shifted. A new pattern has emerged. It's unthinkable. Unacceptable. It goes against every statute you've ever issued," he cried. "You've got to punish them!"

"I will examine their deeds," Amun-Ra said quietly. "Whether they are punished or not is none of your concern."

"It is the concern of all of us!" he shouted in response.

A meek voice echoed in the chamber. "Perhaps Seth needs to witness this," Nephthys said, and Isis turned, considering her sister. Nephthys knew something. Something she wasn't sharing.

Amun-Ra, too, lifted his gaze to Nephthys and studied her silently. After a moment, he nodded. "Very well. You may stay," he said to Seth. Then he shifted on his throne, giving his full attention to the two who stood in front of him, hands clasped. Amun-Ra frowned. "Who would like to go first?" he asked.

Isis was about to speak when Osiris took a step forward. "I love Isis," he declared boldly, and Isis's heart warmed at his words, feeling the truth of them echo in her frame. "We have enacted a spell so that we can be together."

Amun-Ra leaned forward. "And it's a powerful one at that." He cocked his head. "Where did this spell come from?"

"I created it," Isis volunteered.

"Can it be undone?"

A chill stole through Isis, and she opened her mouth but found she couldn't speak. The very idea of dissolving the connection between her and Osiris was as abhorrent to her now as cutting off her own arm.

Nephthys answered the question. "It cannot. The pattern of the stars has been rewritten, the laws altered."

Isis swallowed and shot her sister a grateful look, but then Nephthys added, "There is no . . . unmaking what has been done."

Taking in a startled breath, Isis glanced surreptitiously at Seth, and her jaw tightened when she saw his small smirk and his bold perusal of her. *Let him try,* she thought.

"I see," Amun-Ra said. He sat back on his throne and rubbed his jaw as he considered his options.

There was a long pause, and all eyes turned to the great god. Finally, he sighed. "Will you promise not to have children?" he queried.

"Do . . . do you mean for us to remain as gods?" Osiris asked incredulously.

"What did you think I was going to do?" Amun-Ra asked.

"Make us mortal," Osiris responded.

Amun-Ra gave a half laugh. "I'm not sure I could even if I wanted to. Besides, we still have need of your various abilities," he said with a wave of his hand, indicating them both. "You didn't answer my question. Do you intend to have children?"

Osiris was about to answer when Isis stilled him with the press of her hand on his arm. "We promise that we will not bring new life into this world without your knowledge."

Amun-Ra considered Isis's words and then gave a final nod. "Then it would seem we have a wedding feast to plan."

The elation that Isis and Osiris felt at the

announcement was tempered by Seth's outburst. "What?" he cried. "Is this the protocol now? The gods can marry each other at will as long as they promise not to procreate?"

Amun-Ra grunted. "The law has been rewritten. What they've done applies to us all," he said with a stony gaze.

Nephthys stepped forward and asked softly, "Can you not try to find the good in this, Seth?"

Seth paused, his anger ebbing as he considered the pleading expression on her face. He seemed to reach some kind of decision, for he tucked his hands behind his back, gave Nephthys a brief nod, spat a sarcastic "Congratulations" to the couple, and took his leave.

"There," Amun-Ra said. "Now that the unpleasantness is over, I'll announce to the city that there is a wedding party tonight. Nephthys?"

"Yes?"

"You'll see to the details?"

"Of course," she answered with a demure nod.

"But wait," Isis said as Amun-Ra rose to leave. "I must speak with you about Seth."

Nephthys took hold of Isis's arm with a firm grip.

"This is not the time to bother Amun-Ra with trivial news. It's your wedding!"

"But he needs to know . . ."

"Trust me when I say that whatever you want to tell him, Amun-Ra already knows. Besides, it can wait until tomorrow, can't it?"

Isis bit her lip. "Can it, sister?"

Nephthys knew Isis was really asking her to use her second sight. Trying to look confident, Nephthys answered, "I'm certain. The stars have reignited. They burn in new ways now than they once did, but they still whisper to me, and their message is that all will be well."

Nephthys knew that her sister might never forgive her for hiding what was coming, but she also knew that what was going to be was supposed to be. Everything depended on it. Nephthys wasn't aware of all the details of what would come to pass, not exactly, but she was aware that great sorrow would rest upon her sister's shoulders tonight.

Still, she would make everything as beautiful for her sister as she could. Nephthys didn't want her to miss even a moment of the happiness she sought. For that reason, Nephthys sent Isis and Osiris away to rest while she prepared, not only for their wedding feast, but for what else awaited them.

Servants came, including Baniti, who was brought up to Heliopolis specifically to distract Isis. Osiris insisted that his lovely new wife needed to spend the day recuperating from her spell, and as tired as Isis was, she didn't protest. She allowed Baniti to spirit her off and help her into a fragrant tub scented with Egyptian oil. Isis took comfort in the fact that she knew exactly what her new husband was doing and where he was at all times. Even when she slept, her thoughts intertwined with Osiris's, and both were comforted despite their physical separation.

* * *

Meanwhile, Seth had journeyed to the mortal world and stood at the edge of a vast and ancient forest—the largest and deepest of any on the entire planet. It was one of which Osiris was particularly proud and to which he often journeyed to bring back plant samples as well as various creatures to add to his menagerie. Flexing his fingers, Seth seethed and paced.

How could this have happened without my knowledge? he wondered irascibly. His angry thoughts were a hailstorm pummeling the Earth, each vengeful idea bouncing wildly off the next. The air smelled of living things—tree sap, spruce, and pine—and a fine white mist blanketed the ground, giving the forest an air of mystery. Birds and small animals hopped from branch to moss-covered branch, filling the air with their happy song over the union.

Seth hated everything about the forest. The trees mocked him, standing thick-trunked and tall. Proud and immovable. Just like Osiris. As he stared into the shadows of the trees, Seth felt something dark and slithering unfurl inside him. It coiled around his heart and squeezed, its jaws unhinging to swallow him whole. Each beat of his heart was startling, as if he stood in a hallway full of doors and each one he tried to enter slammed with a shocking finality, barring his exit. Seth clenched his fists as the cold blackness oozed through his veins, daring him to move against it.

But then, instead of straining against the leviathan that had taken hold of his mind and heart, he stilled and allowed it to take root. As it circled and spread, he remained unmoving. He stood like a scarecrow, hollow and stiff-limbed, the sun bleaching him of any vestiges of sympathy or kindness.

When the darkness finally settled in him like a sleeping dragon, Seth moved. His heart was now a cold, black millstone—unbending, unyielding, and unfeeling. If he was not to be honored, then he would be feared. Determination burned in his body, melting any remaining doubts away like waxy tallow.

Raising his hands, he channeled his vast power, stretching himself further than he ever had before. He felt no pride in the act of unmaking, no fear of the consequences, only a sense of vindication. Thick tree roots erupted from the ground, creating a dense morass of wood that splintered and pushed until the trees fell and then disappeared, shrinking into the giant holes that had been their beds.

Soon all that was left were gaping wounds where the great soldiers of the forest had once stood. The remaining vegetation slouched over the empty pockets, half uprooted and fluttering like the lips of a toothless old man.

Moving forward, Seth worked. The ferns rolled in

on themselves until they became dust and scattered in the wind. The clumps of delicate lichen and moss shriveled as if he'd set them on fire. They blackened and disappeared until even the smell of fungus, sap, and wood was obliterated. When he was done with the flora, Seth turned his attention to the fauna.

Larger animals cried out, the beasts lumbering haphazardly across the now alien terrain, completely oblivious to predator or prey as they searched for their lost homes. Closing his eyes, he unmade them all. Some quickly. Some slowly. Smaller creatures that had hidden in the remains of the plants scampered haphazardly into holes and burrowed in the dirt. Flocks of birds darted this way and that in chaotic patterns, often bumping into each other as if confused.

The vast numbers of creatures startled Seth, and yet he felt no remorse over their demise. Power filled his frame as he eradicated them, first as small groups and then by herds and swarms, until not even the tiniest ant remained. The blood and carnage that had stained the land with his slower unmakings was now gone. Gravity no longer had hold over him as he channeled his thoughts and rose into the air, scanning the vast plain before him for any remaining organisms, and found nothing but a river devoid of life.

White streams of water fell across the rocks, spilling like a woman's hair over the arm of the one she loved. The thought caused a certain melancholy to steal over Seth. Irritated, he moved on to the deep pool the waterfall fed and sat upon a rock as he stared at his reflection. He should have been proud of the way he looked. Coming into his power had added a bronze glow of health to his skin and a full thickness to his hair, and had strengthened his frame. But the handsome face staring back at him seemed to mock him. It didn't matter that his image had changed. He still hated what he saw.

Seth let out a heavy sigh, set aside his recent failure, and focused on how he could accomplish his goals, as well as what he should do about Isis's abandonment. His mind stilled until his thoughts were as flat and motionless as the water's surface. Then, with only the noise of the moving water as his companion, he plotted his next move.

When he was satisfied with his machinations, he rose, and to his delight found he was able to unmake the river as well. His mother immediately began crying at what he'd done, her clouds gathering overhead. He cocked his head as he realized that the water had been a part of her and that what he'd done had, in essence, been like cutting off a piece of her.

The idea that he could indeed harm a god, even one as powerful as his mother, filled him with happiness. The fat drops of her rain annoying him, he waved his hand and was gratified to feel her retreat from him completely. The ground rumbled as his father responded to the injury he'd caused his mother, but Seth ignored him.

The morning sun was only a handbreadth above the horizon as Seth turned in a slow circle to study his work. The vast forest of Osiris was now a barren desert that stretched as far as the eye could see. Not a drop of water existed within its bounds, and even his mother would think twice about raining upon it now. Rising into the air, he headed back to Heliopolis. There was much to do before he attended the reception that evening; the first task would require him to be his most charming self so as to distract the one planning the party.

* * *

It proved easier than he thought. With the moon a glowing

backdrop, Seth entered Amun-Ra's home with a beautiful yet subdued Nephthys on his arm, which he deemed most appropriate. Seth and Nephthys swept into the feast and he was gratified that all eyes turned to him, even the goddess he'd lost to the one he loathed above all others.

"Seth," Amun-Ra said with a small smile that didn't reach his eyes. "So happy you could join us."

"I see the feast has started without us," Seth said.

Isis rose. "We weren't sure you were coming." The tone of the goddess was one of wariness but also confusion, especially as she noticed her sister's arm resting upon Seth's. "The feasting is over," she said. "I'm sorry you had to miss it," she added, pointedly looking at the sister who'd arranged everything.

"I was . . . busy," Nephthys explained without telling them anything.

Amun-Ra frowned and stepped forward, offering his arm to Nephthys. "We're still happy to see you here," he said, more to her than to Seth. "Perhaps you would consider helping me start the dancing, Nephthys?"

"What a wonderful idea," Seth said with sneer. "Since we missed the feast, the least my new wife and I can do is to celebrate the marriage of the gods with a dance. Shall we, my dear?"

Nephthys bit her lip as Amun-Ra raised his hand and the music suddenly came to a stop. "What did you say?" Amun-Ra asked. "I fear I misheard you."

Seth leaned forward. "You didn't. Nephthys and I have been recently married."

"You what?" Isis approached and grabbed her sister's arm, pulling her away. "Is he telling the truth?" she demanded.

"He is," Nephthys said. "We were wed just an hour ago."

Isis gaped in shock, stepping back and letting go as if she'd become infected with whatever it was that had possessed her sister.

Amun-Ra took her place and had no such hesitation about touching Nephthys. Almost tenderly, he took hold of her shoulder. "Were you coerced?" he asked softly.

Nephthys's eyes gleamed with unshed tears as she looked up into Amun-Ra's face. "No," she answered. "When he asked me, I agreed." Stepping closer, she whispered so that only Amun-Ra could hear, "My light will bring him balance."

Amun-Ra studied her carefully. "Do you love him, then?" he asked, and everyone waited with bated breath to hear her reply.

But before she could answer, Seth stepped between them. "Of course she does. And if you're thinking of dissolving our union, you'd first have to undo whatever it is the two of them have done," he said, pointing to Isis and Osiris. "But I'll remind you that just this morning you said as long as there was no"—he waved his hand distractedly—"procreating going on, such a union was acceptable."

Amun-Ra took a step back. "Yes . . . ," he agreed slowly. "That I did."

"Then you don't see a reason that the two of us can't be married?"

Folding his arms across his broad chest, Amun-Ra answered, "If Nephthys entered this . . . arrangement of her own free will and choice, then I won't protest it."

"Good," Seth said with a cheeky smirk. "Then I'd say we should get on with the party. Shall we dance, wife?"

Nephthys shot Amun-Ra an indiscernible look,

then nodded and followed her new husband to the dance floor. The stunned musicians hurried to resume their interrupted song. Despite the fact that Nephthys had planned the festivities with excruciating attention to detail, none of those involved felt much like celebrating any longer. Osiris drew Isis aside and whispered in her ear while Seth twirled Nephthys to the music that now sounded jarring and shrill to Isis, despite the fact that they were the most talented musical group Osiris had ever found. Amun-Ra quickly made his excuses and left, an ember of regret in his eyes.

The party continued, but the only one who seemed happy was Seth, who accepted the halfhearted congratulations of those in attendance with relish.

When a few of the citizens of Heliopolis apologized profusely for bringing a gift only for Isis and Osiris and not for him and his new bride, he laughed away their concerns as if such a thing was of no importance. Nephthys bobbed her head in agreement and joined her sister as Isis unwrapped her gifts, trying to make up for the fact that she'd done the unthinkable on her sister's wedding day.

Standing by her sister's side, she read the notes

from well-wishers and exclaimed over gifts as if nothing amiss was going on. Seth disappeared for a time and Isis tried to smile, but her eyes kept darting over to her sister. *What was she thinking? How could she have married Seth!* She kept waiting for a chance to draw her sister aside and tell her what she knew of her new husband, but before she could, Seth entered the hall again. This time he was with a dozen servants bearing a beautiful box of gold.

"What is this?" Nephthys asked Seth as her husband approached.

"It's my gift for the happy couple. A little token to show them exactly what they mean to me."

"How . . . lovely," Nephthys said as she pasted a grin on her face.

Isis hadn't missed the line that had appeared between her sister's arched brows. She didn't know what was going on, but if there was one person in the world she trusted as much as she did her new husband, it was her sister. At least, she thought she could still trust her. "Nephthys?" Isis said, the question in her mind not needing to be voiced.

Nephthys gave a small nod, so Isis let out a breath and took hold of her husband's arm. "Thank you for thinking of us," she said to Seth stiffly.

"Not at all," he replied with a crocodile leer. "I wanted to gift you with something that shows my absolute regard."

The heavy box was set down before Osiris, and he waved a hand indicating that Osiris should open it. The lid creaked as they did so, and Seth could not withhold the delight on his face as he watched their reactions.

Osiris frowned. "What is this?" he asked, stooping to examine the contents.

Seth practically cackled in glee. "Don't you recognize it?"

"Sand?" Isis said.

"Not at all," Seth answered. "You see, I've brought you your favorite spot in all the cosmos. And what's more, I wrapped it all up in a neat little package." In a stage whisper he murmured, "Think of it as a souvenir from the place you were planning to go on your honeymoon." Sighing, Seth shook his head. "I see the two of you need me to spell it out. This"—he indicated, sweeping his hand through the grains—"is your beloved forest."

"What?" Osiris asked in disbelief. "How can this

be?"

"Isis knows. Don't you, Isis?"

Her face paled and she swallowed before speaking. "You *unmade* an entire forest?"

"Not just *a* forest, *the* forest. The one he spends all his time in," he said, jerking his thumb at Osiris. "Clearly the two of you should have talked more before marrying. I find it truly shocking that you don't know his most treasured places."

"You unmade it?" Osiris asked again, understanding and horror filling him.

The love he held for the place was akin to Isis's love for Baniti; she could feel the pain of it reverberating through him. As she turned to her husband to offer him what comfort she could, she heard Seth say, "That's not all I'll unmake."

Osiris sank to his knees and slowly dipped his fingers into the box, scooping up a handful of sand, letting the granules trickle through his fingers. It took several seconds for him to realize that his fingertips were also dissolving. He looked up at Seth. "What have you done?" he demanded.

Seth crouched down, his eyes burning with

intensity as he channeled the stolen energies of thousands of living creatures that roiled in his frame. "You stupid, stubborn immortal. Perhaps if you had known that I would grow to have more power than all of you, you might have treated me better. You're finally getting what you deserve."

Leaning closer so that only Osiris could hear him, Seth whispered, "Isis will be mine. I will take her to the desert where your forest once stood. There she will vow to belong to me and me alone. You will be nothing more to her then than these grains of sand to be cast beneath her feet."

"No!" Isis cried. "Nephthys, help me!"

"There's nothing I can do!" Nephthys said as tears fell heavily onto her cheeks.

Osiris's arm began to melt away, and then his chest caved in as more grains of sand lifted from his body and fell into the golden box. Quickly, Osiris spun toward his wife. "Isis," he pleaded. "Remember, I love you."

"Osiris!" Isis knelt down, encircling her husband in her arms as if she could hold him together by will alone. He pressed his lips to hers in a final kiss, but all she felt was the sting of sand as he dissolved in front of her eyes.

The remnants of his being floated into the box and settled.

Crying out, Isis took hold of the golden box and began chanting a spell, but no matter how she tried to weave the words together, her power seemed to elude her. She needed time. Grabbing a fistful of sand, she staggered to her feet. Nephthys took her arm to support her. "You're a monster," Isis spat at the gloating man standing before her.

Seth smiled coolly. "A monster of your making, my dear. You should have said yes when I asked you to choose me. Now you'll end up with nothing unless you do exactly as I say."

Isis wove a spell to incapacitate him, channeling as much power as she could muster, but Seth just laughed and tugged at his shirt to show her a gleaming red stone hanging around his neck.

"Your spells, as much as I appreciate them, cannot affect me when I wear the celestial bloodstone."

"Where did you get that?" Isis demanded. There was only one living person left in all of the cosmos who would know what could bind Isis's power. Isis prayed she was wrong.

"Why, your lovely sister, of course," he said, and

Isis closed her eyes, wishing she could unhear his response. Seth went on, "She knew you'd want revenge for the loss of Osiris. It's only right that she'd want to protect her new husband."

Isis wrenched her arm away from Nephthys, her eyes stinging with betrayal and loss. *How could this be possible? To lose my beloved and my sister all in one day?*

Nephthys tried to speak, but Isis held up her hand. "No. Don't you dare say a word."

Seth clucked his tongue. "Poor Isis. It would seem that despite his immortal nature, your new husband has been visited by death. How distressing. How . . . impossible. And yet here I am, recently invigorated by the remains of your former husband's life energy, and fortunately for you, still eager to embrace you as a wife. Of course, now you'll be relegated to the status of second wife, but I promise to give you an equal amount of attention."

"You're sick," Isis hissed. "I'll never accept you!"

His smile disappeared and he took a threatening step forward, all the darkness inside him apparent in his demeanor. "And you're foolish if you think to thwart me again." Seth grabbed Isis's wrist, painfully jerking her toward him, and whispered in her ear. "Think about what else you have to lose," he threatened cunningly.

Tears streaming down her face, Isis looked at her sister and then at Baniti, who stood at the edge of the room, her eyes wide in terror as she pressed her hands to her mouth. Isis did think about what else she had to lose, but in that moment nothing was as important as the grains of sand trickling between her clenched fingers. Eyes bright with determination, she took a deep breath and whispered a spell. Her spells might have had no effect on Seth, but they still worked on her.

A ray of moonlight stole through the window, the light bending until it fell upon Isis. Reaching out, she took hold of the light and used its power to shift her form until her body appeared almost ghostlike and she was able to slip from Seth's grasp. Alarmed, he tried to take hold of her again, but his hands passed through her as if she were no longer corporeal.

Clutching the sand that was once her husband, Isis leapt upon the moonbeam and it sped her far, far away from Heliopolis. But despite the moonlight that bore her up to the stars, the heaviness of her sorrow reminded her that the distance between her and her beloved now was something even the stars couldn't breach.

CHAPTER 7

UPROOTED

Isis didn't know how long she floated there, alone, mourning the love she'd only just won. Her tears flowed freely, her great sorrow provoking the stars to weep as well. The drops fell to the mortal realm and caused the already swollen Nile to rise higher than it ever had before, flooding the countryside so that all who lived within its bounds knew that something terrible must have happened to prevent Osiris from protecting them as he usually did.

She heard the flap of wings and felt the brush of air against her skin. It was Nephthys. Isis's sorrow turned to rage. "Leave me!" she demanded. "Go back to your husband. The two of you deserve each other."

"I will not abandon you," Nephthys replied coolly.

Isis gaped at her incredulously. "Abandon me? You've already abandoned me. Betrayed me for one who has done the unthinkable! How could you support such a thing? Tell me you didn't see this in a vision. Tell me I'm wrong. Tell me you could have done nothing to prevent it."

Not until that moment did Isis truly understand the depths of Nephthys's deception. It was written all over her face. Regret and sorrow swam in Nephthys's eyes, confirming her suspicions. Her sister had seen this play out in a vision. Had seen it and had done nothing to prevent it. "I cannot abide to look at you," Isis said as she turned away.

"Isis, stop." Nephthys put a hand on her sister's shoulder. "I know there is much damage I must repair between us, but there is too much to be done and there isn't enough time for me to explain. Just know that all of these things, including the death of your husband, had to come to pass for the cosmos to be in balance."

Despite her need to leave, Isis paused to ask one

final question. "How can anything ever be in balance again if Osiris is gone?"

"He's not gone, sister."

"What?" Isis spun around. "What do you mean?"

Nephthys blew out a breath. "He's still here. Can't you feel him?"

"Feel him? How?"

"It was your spell. You are still connected. Even now. If you want to bring him back, we must hurry."

"But Seth . . ."

"Forget about Seth for the time being. Do you want your husband back or don't you?"

Isis blinked, and the air stirred by Nephthys's wings dried the tears that stung her eyes. "Of course I want him back," she murmured, confusion obvious on her face.

"Then follow me," Nephthys demanded cryptically, leaving no quarter for further inquiries.

Isis took to the sky, trailing after her sister as a million questions surfaced in her mind. *Can it be true? Is it possible that Osiris is still within my reach?* Nephthys flew swiftly, and Isis was surprised when Mount Babel came into view. When Isis angled toward the base of the mountain, Nephthys banked until she drew close to her sister. Taking hold of her hand, she said, "The stars allow me passage now. If you hold on to me, the path will be clear."

The sisters alit on the pinnacle of the mountain in the exact spot where Isis had woven her spell—the place she now held sacred, where she'd united with Osiris not a day before.

Nephthys knelt on the surface of the great adder stone and tucked her wings behind her back, indicating for Isis to follow suit. Gently, she pried open her sister's hand and scooped the sand into a small pile between them, shaping it so that it had four sides and rose to a peak in the middle, forming a pyramid. "Do you have his true name?" Nephthys asked.

Isis nodded.

"Then we will use it to summon him back from the Waters of Chaos. Cast a spell, sister," she urged. "Create a body for him from his dusty remains. The power of the cosmos will light the pyramid from within, and when it does, use your memory of him to shape his new form. Then, when we are ready, we will use his true name to guide him to it and your shared hearts will reunite."

Isis began weaving the spell. She'd never done one like it before, and it took several attempts, but at last the cosmos responded. Light bloomed within the sand as she chanted, and her spell became a song. It was rich and full of the love she felt for Osiris. Music was such an important part of him that singing the spell felt right.

Nephthys joined her voice to her sister's, and to Isis's delight, she heard the echo of Osiris's heartbeat. It was almost too faint even for her to hear, but it gave her hope. Hours passed as the women sang, and the sand shifted in response. It stretched and pulsed, forming the vague outline of a man, and then her song carved the planes of his chest, his strong arms, and finally, the angles of his handsome face.

When the grains settled and the light dissipated, she saw that the framework of her husband was perfect down to the last tiny detail, but he was not breathing. Instead of flesh and bone, the sand had hardened into polished stone, and she could not sense that his heart was any nearer than it had been when she started.

Collapsing, Isis panted. "What did I do wrong?" she besought.

"Nothing. We'll just need some help for the next

step."

Seeing Isis slouching in defeat, Nephthys squeezed her sister's hands then let go and stood. "Rest for a time. I will fetch Anubis. He will bake the stone with the fires of immortality and then the form will take on flesh."

When Isis reached desperately for her sister, taking hold of her arm, Nephthys understood the reason. "I will only bring Anubis, I promise you."

Isis nodded, now left alone with the burnished replica of her husband. Osiris's hands were folded across his chest and his eyes were closed. She curved her body over his, brushing away some lingering grains of sand from his cheek and trailing her fingertips over the hard line of his jaw. She longed for him to wake, to wrap her in his arms and assure her that he wouldn't leave her again.

Isis.

She jerked and realized she must have been sleeping, slumped over his likeness for a time. Had he tried to contact her?

Pressing her hands to the bronzed face, she spoke. "Can you hear me, husband?" she asked, full of bright-eyed, desperate anticipation. "Osiris?" she called. There was no answer.

A lone tear splashed onto his chest, and Isis swiped at her eyes. When she looked down at the spot where it had fallen, she gasped. The wet spots on his chest and bare shoulder had become warm, and the color changed to match Osiris's own golden bronze tone. But to her disappointment, she watched as the soft spot she stroked with her thumb slowly changed back to polished stone. Try as she might, she could not replicate the miracle.

When Nephthys returned, Anubis just behind her, Isis spoke excitedly of her discovery.

"There is power in your tears, sister. Your connection to Osiris has allowed a teardrop to form from the Waters of Chaos." Nephthys stepped aside, indicating Anubis should take her place. "Unfortunately, not even you could muster enough tears to give his form flesh." Nephthys put her hand on Anubis's shoulder. "You know what to do," she told him.

"I have never done this before," he said. "There's no precedent."

"Just because it hasn't been done before does not mean such a thing is impossible," she replied. "Allow the stars to guide you." Nephthys remained unwavering even as he gave her a doubt-filled look.

Crouching down, Anubis placed a hand on Isis's arm. "I'll do what I can, goddess."

"Thank you," Isis whispered, and shifted back to give him room.

Anubis began chanting. His words resonated with power as he rebuked drought and darkness, storms and chaos—all the things Osiris was the antithesis of. While he did so, Isis fidgeted, clamping her hands together, pinching her lips, and fluttering her wings in a rhythmic pattern, as if to soothe the anguish she felt. When the fire took hold of Osiris's form, she stood back. The heat of a thousand suns blazed, baking him, and through the flames, Isis saw the polished stone melt into soft flesh.

"It worked," Anubis said with delight. When he lowered his hands, the flames banked and extinguished, but the flesh began to change back to stone in the same manner it had when Isis's tear dried. Anubis lifted his arms again to bring back the flame. When it dissipated, his arms shook. "You'll have to hurry," he said. "Seth's power continues to unmake him."

"Only when the breath of life returns and he is in command of his body again can you let go of the immortal flame," Nephthys explained. Then she urged, "Call him, sister. Now that he is flesh, the path is clear. Bid him return and graft his true self to this new body."

"Osiris, my love," Isis cried. "My heart calls to you. Come back to me. I summon you. Traverse the cosmos. Find me!"

Isis knelt, ignoring the heat of his body, and placed her palms on Osiris's chest. Closing her eyes, she leaned over, relishing the feel of his soft hair against her cheek, and whispered his true name in his ear. Immediately she felt a jolt in her heart, and the piece of him that resided with her responded.

"He comes!" Nephthys shouted.

Isis looked up and saw a tiny pinprick of light zoom toward them. It slowed when it neared, hesitating, and then it finally sank into Osiris's chest just where his heart would be. The body glowed as if lit from the inside with a celestial light, but unlike Anubis's flame, this light carried no heat. The skeleton and muscles of the god were outlined clearly through his flesh. Tiny plants sprouted all around the form, a sure sign that the god of growing things had returned.

But then, just as Isis allowed the flame of hope to

fill her as well, the light inside Osiris's body dimmed and retreated from his limbs, first at his fingertips and then his arms. The seedlings shrank and shriveled, turning brown and dying before her eyes.

"Quickly!" Nephthys cried. "Do not let his life essence escape!"

She knelt by Osiris's head and told Isis to kneel at his feet. Together they raised their wings and prevented the orb of light that had risen from the body from fleeing. It bounced against their soft feathers, trying to return to the Waters of Chaos. "Sing him back into his body again, Isis!"

The goddess lifted her voice and the tiny orb drifted closer to her, hovering near her before entering the inert form again.

"Keep singing and stir the air with your wings. It brings life," Nephthys instructed, and then she turned to the god standing next to her. "Anubis, I need your help. We must bind his life essence to his new form."

"What do I need to do?"

"I cannot leave my position. You must use your scythe to take our hair."

"You want me to cut it off?" His brows knitted in

confusion.

"Yes. Then you need to wrap it around him. Every part of him will need to be bound. You'll have to take it all."

Anubis hesitated for only a moment. Raising his scythe, he sheared off Isis's hair, then moved behind Nephthys and did the same. Gathering fistfuls of their long hair, he wrapped Osiris's body with the soft locks, tying it off in knots as he did so. When every part of Osiris's new body had been encased, Nephthys instructed, "Now whisper his true name again, sister."

Isis obeyed. The light spread, filling the newly made form once again, but this time it glowed brighter and brighter until the rays of it burst from between the strands of hair and dissolved it. When the light faded, Nephthys said, "It is done. Come, Anubis, we will leave them alone."

"But he's still not breathing!" Isis cried as Anubis helped Nephthys to her feet.

"The rest is up to you," Nephthys said gently. "When you place your lips on his, the breath of life will enter his new body."

Nephthys staggered as she moved ahead and

leaned heavily on Anubis.

Isis let out a heavy sigh and stared after her sister, resolving to decide what to do about her betrayal later. As they left, Isis's body shook with spasms of deep fatigue. She felt drained as she never had been before. To have wrought two spells of such power in the span of one day would have killed a lesser being, but Isis was determined. All that remained was a kiss. Surely she could muster enough energy for such a small thing.

Kneeling beside her husband, she stroked his soft hair. Her hands trembled as she drew them down to his face. Tilting his head, she gently pressed her lips to his. She tasted the salt of her tears and felt the residual heat from the fires that had baked him. Then there was a rush of wind. The chest beneath her rose and fell.

A hand wrapped around her waist and pulled her closer as his lips moved against hers, first tentatively, then hungrily. Osiris sat up, shifting her with him. Taking hold of her shoulders, he eased away so he could look at her. He wiped away her tears with his thumbs and slid his hand into her shorn hair, his expression thoughtful and sad as the short strands fell through his fingers.

Isis couldn't stop touching him. She caressed his

neck and his powerful shoulders and swept the hair from his eyes. Osiris did the same with her, but then he finally took hold of her fingers and brought them to his lips for a quick kiss.

"I'm here, Little One," he said. "And I won't leave you again."

"How do we know?" she demanded with a sob. "How do we stop Seth's next attempt?"

"Amun-Ra will stop him. We should go now. We'll need his aid if we want to contain Seth."

She nodded and he helped her to her feet. Osiris shifted back and forth, moving his limbs, testing out his new body for the first time. When he was ready to go, Isis said, "Wait."

"What is it?" he asked.

She waved her hand over his chest and a golden chain with a red gemstone appeared.

"What's this?" Osiris asked as he examined it.

"It contains my lifeblood. It ties us together. If he unmakes one of us, he unmakes both." She took a step closer and grasped his hand. "I'll not be separated from you again," she said. "Even if it means my death."

Soberly, he nodded. Then he kissed her and

trailed his fingers over her neck. When he lifted his head, she felt the tickle of a chain. He had created a necklace for her as well. Isis lifted it and saw it was an amulet crafted after the fashion of an Egyptian ankh, but the sides turned down instead. When Isis looked up, he explained.

"It's a tyet—a knot that binds and brings life. These are your arms and your wings when they are wrapped around me," he said. "This"—he tapped the center—"is the kiss that gave me breath. I am bound to you, my love, my Isis. My life is yours. No matter what the future brings."

Isis nodded and her eyes closed, causing her to stumble. Osiris caught her, briefly kissed her lips, and said, "Rest now, Little One. It's my turn to fly."

Lifting his wife in his arms and cradling her close, Osiris called upon the heart scarabs that bound them, relishing in the flutter of her heart that was locked within his chest. He took to the skies, knowing he'd have to confront the most powerful god he'd ever faced and that it might result in the deaths of both of them.

CHAPTER 8

TRANSPLANTED

"Are you sure you need to do this?" Anubis asked.

"He is my husband," Nephthys answered simply, as if that were explanation enough. When she saw Anubis's furrowed forehead and hesitation to leave her side, she placed her hand on his arm. "All will be well, Anubis. Our fates are written in the stars, and my light will not be snuffed out this day."

Still seeing he would not leave her, Nephthys left him instead. Steeling herself, she looked heavenward for just an instant, silently asking her mother to watch over her, to watch over them all, and then entered the chamber. "Seth?" she called.

There was no reply. She surveyed the room

carefully, knowing he was there. Gooseflesh rose on her arms. Finally, she caught sight of a black scorpion tucked beneath a chair. She crouched down. "Ah, there you are."

The small creature scuttled out, its body transforming into a snapping gray crocodile and then to a bristled boar. It shook its head and bellowed, its dangerous tusks nearly spearing her leg, but Nephthys didn't move. Didn't even raise an eyebrow.

When he settled into his own natural form, she asked, "How many other species have you exterminated this day, that you can take their shape so easily?"

Seth folded his arms across his chest while his nostrils flared. "Let's see," he answered with a mix of pride and mockery. "A woolly hippo, the desert bull, and the white-tailed oryx, which, incidentally, I unmade just to pass the time, which was entirely your fault. A wife shouldn't leave her husband on their wedding night."

"And a husband shouldn't commit murder on his."

Seth's eyes darted to hers. "You knew what I was going to do when you agreed to accompany me to their celebration, didn't you, my little visionary?"

Nephthys stared at him stonily, her lips pressed

into a tight line. Instead of answering him, she asked, "Does it give you pleasure to cause such wanton destruction?"

A small sigh escaped him and he looked away.

Do I see regret there? she wondered.

He spoke softly, but there was an underlying hardness to his tone. "Despite what you might think, no, destruction and chaos bring me no pleasure. They are a means to an end. There is purpose in what I have done. But you know that better than anyone, don't you, little wife?" Seth seized her arm and drew her toward him to stroke the short hair away from her face roughly. "I don't like what you've done with your hair, by the way." Pressing his palms against her cheeks, he squeezed. Not tightly enough to hurt her, but there was no escaping his grasp either.

Seth's gaze drifted to her mouth, and before she could react, he kissed her. His lips moved against hers in a hungry, powerful, and dominating fashion. He seemed surprised when she responded to him. His kiss softened then, and Nephthys trembled with the knowledge of what the two of them could be, would be, if what the stars told her came to pass. But then he abruptly ended it, wrenching himself back as if she was a temptation that he wanted to thrust as far away from himself as possible.

A line appeared between his brows but it vanished with a smirk, twisting his otherwise handsome face into something ugly and cruel. Seth took hold of her chin. "Now. Are you going to share your secrets with me, or am I going to take them? I promise you that I'll enjoy it either way."

Nephthys jerked her chin from his grip and stepped back. "How quickly you have discarded your cloak of charm."

With flashing eyes he said, "You knew what I was. You've always known. I think it's time that both of us stop pretending to be something we are not."

"Perhaps you are right," she said with a demure nod.

Seth's eyes bored into hers as if willing her to spill her secrets. He paced a few steps away and then returned. "Tell me what you have seen."

"You're not ready to hear all of what I've seen."

"Do you think to deny me?" Seth took hold of her arms and tugged her close. "We are wed, Nephthys," he murmured. "Submitting to your husband goes hand in hand with making vows. You and your visions belong to me now. Lest my willful wife forget, marrying was her idea."

"Yes," Nephthys admitted. "I wanted to marry you."

Seth lifted an eyebrow. "That much I know. What escapes me are your motives."

Nephthys was quiet for a moment, and when Seth seemed content to let her go, she stepped away again. She found it interesting that despite his obvious resistance to being close to her, he kept coming back, as if he couldn't help it.

After considering a moment, she let out a soft sigh. "You are right that there is not enough energy left in the Waters of Chaos. The gift you wield is an important one, and one not to be dismissed. Your power is necessary to bring balance. It is just as important to the care of the cosmos as is Amun-Ra's."

He blinked, astonishment evident on his face.

Quickly, she continued, "But your power, if wielded incorrectly, will destroy us all." Nephthys nibbled on her bottom lip and then came to a decision. Reaching out, she took his hand. "Seth, I am sorry for the suffering you've borne and for the loneliness you've felt. I know you are a man of great ability. You are clever and passionate, but as of late your passion has turned into obsession and jealousy."

Seth's face went blank and Nephthys shivered.

"You need to know that Osiris lives," she said bravely. When he didn't stir, she pressed on. "You have not destroyed him as you intended. Isis has created a new body for him, and their bond has allowed him to return. I know you hate him. His booming laugh feels like mockery. When you see them together it hurts you. You feel diminished when he is near. I also know you think you love Isis, but if you saw them together you'd understand that she can only be happy with him. She will never feel the same way for you."

"He lives?" Seth demanded her confirmation with feverish eyes.

"Yes, but you're missing the point."

"And what point is that, dear wife?"

"That it's a good thing. You haven't gone too far that you can't come back. Amun-Ra will forgive this. What you've done has been fixed. I fixed it for you." The smile she gave him was too forced to be natural.

A muscle twitched in his jaw and she hurried to finish.

"I beg you, Seth, walk away from this path. I know what motivates you. You crave acceptance. To be respected, valued, and loved. You desire the admiration that has been long denied you and wish to feel as if your opinions matter just as much as everyone else's. You will get all of those things. I promise you. All you have to do is bide your time."

"And why should I wait when I have already waited so long? Why should I put faith in your visions? Trust you? Especially when I can see that you do not hold me in the same esteem as you do the others. You look down upon me, too. Don't deny it."

Nephthys hesitated, unsure of what to say. Carefully, gently, she proceeded. "You are right," she confessed. "Though I do not love you as a wife should a husband, the stars have shown me that there will come a time when I do. Someday we will be very happy together, the cosmos will be harmonious, and all the desires of your heart will be yours. Surely with that end in sight, you can find the strength within you to be patient with the others, to give me time to become the wife you need. Let Isis and

Osiris have their happiness, husband."

Nephthys fell silent as she stared into Seth's hooded gaze. Finally, he spoke. "My earnest bride," he began, stretching out his fingers to stroke her feathers, "I want to thank you for sharing your feelings. I can tell they come from your heart. But you are wrong. Your visions have misled you. Not about me. All the things I want, will, of course, come to pass, but it won't happen if I sit back and rest upon my laurels.

"I'm done begging for castoffs, favors, and leftovers. The lesson the cosmos has taught me over and over is that the only way to obtain something I want is to take it. No one is going to be kind enough to simply hand it to me. So, yes, I *will* rule. The cosmos *will* be in harmony. And you *will* become the wife I need. If I have to shape you, fashion you into becoming what I want, then I will."

Seth ran his fingertips from her ear down to her jaw. "You should know that I don't blame you at all for being envious of my feelings toward Isis."

"No." Nephthys shook her head. "That's not what I—"

Seth had leaned down during her protest and cut her off. "But you should be," he murmured in her ear with a seductive voice. "I will always desire her more than you. You will know what it is to be the second choice. The one left behind. Still, you are powerful, and I aim to use your power as I see fit. After all, why should I content myself with one wife, one goddess, when I can have two?"

Hot tears stung the back of Nephthys's eyes as she tried not to allow his hurtful words to take root in her heart. "But Osiris— " she started.

"Can be unmade again," he said with a sneer. "In fact, I should thank you. Unmaking him a second time will prove an interesting experiment. Perhaps this time I will gain even more of his power." Seth touched the tip of her nose. "Already the rumors of my power spread. The people of Heliopolis begin to fear me. Soon they will see that I am the most potent of the gods. They will forget all about Amun-Ra."

"You aren't stronger than him."

"Maybe not yet. But after I unmake all of the other gods, we'll see who has the upper hand."

Nephthys shivered. It gave Seth pleasure to know that she feared him also. That was much better. He didn't like thinking that she knew more than he did. He wouldn't ever allow her to think she was in control.

"Of course," he continued, "you are aware that I must punish you appropriately for having gone behind my back. It simply won't do to have all of Heliopolis know that I have no authority over my wife."

Nephthys straightened stiffly as he strode arrogantly in a circle around her, assessing her from every angle. The color drained from her face and her lower lip quivered. She knew exactly what was coming. She'd hoped that her words might sway him to pursue a different course, but in her heart of hearts she knew that there was no diverting him from his desires. Her eyelids drooped and she gathered her wings around her as if to shield herself from what he was going to do.

Seth then murmured the words that would change her forever, and she gasped at the loss even as it happened. The cut was brutal and swift, the pain of it more psychological than physical, and yet her nerve endings tingled as if a sharp knife still rested upon her skin. Her eyes swam with tears, and she pressed her palms against her face to quell the sobs that racked her frame.

"There, there," Seth said, with a pitying look as he pulled her hands from her face and roughly swept away the tears. "It's your own fault, you know."

"How could you?" Nephthys asked, her voice catching.

His eyes sparked with righteous indignation. "I didn't want to, Nephthys. You forced my hand. It's a shame, too." Leaning closer, he murmured, "Your wings were the only thing I found beautiful about you."

Her expression dulled. "I would think that someone who has suffered so much at the hands of others would have more compassion."

Seth grunted. "Yes, well . . . perhaps next time you'll think twice before attempting to thwart me."

Turning, he flexed his hands, shaking them out as if he'd touched something unpleasant, and strode toward the door.

"I wasn't thwarting you," Nephthys countered softly at his retreating back. "I was saving you."

If he heard her, he didn't acknowledge it.

Nephthys crumpled to the floor, and it was there Amun-Ra found her.

His angry expression blazed with the light of a thousand suns as he gathered her in his arms. "He will die for this," Amun-Ra promised.

Nephthys pressed a palm against his cheek. "No.

He cannot. Not yet. We need him."

Gently, Amun-Ra lifted her and carried her slight form to a settee. Instead of placing her upon it, he settled against the soft cushions himself, positioning her so she lay against him. His arms were strong, and she rested her cheek against his chest. He didn't speak until her fresh tears subsided.

"Tell me what we must do," he said.

"He'll go after Osiris," she said faintly. "If we remove him from Seth's sight, he will focus his energy on pursuing Isis."

"He will threaten her," Amun-Ra said. "Bend her to his will."

"You will limit his reach. As long as he believes he can rightfully persuade her with charm, it will provide sufficient distraction."

"And if she succumbs?"

"She will not. Her love for her husband is sure."

"Let us hope you are right. Together they could accomplish Seth's desires."

"Seth's desires are not those of Isis." She turned her face up to his, and Amun-Ra's breath caught. Wet tears clung to her dark lashes. He had never thought her so beautiful. Even with her shorn hair and without her glorious wings, Nephthys was lovely.

"And what is it that she desires?" Amun-Ra asked huskily.

"What all women desire," she replied. "A man who loves her above all else. Who would sacrifice everything for her."

"You deserve such a man, too," he said.

Reaching up, Nephthys traced the arch of the great god's brow. "And I will have him someday."

Amun-Ra frowned. He wished she trusted him enough to share what she knew. She startled him from his thoughts when she said, "You must allow Isis to have the other wish of her heart."

"What wish is that?"

"A child."

"No." He shook his head. "You know why this is forbidden."

"Nevertheless. He must be born."

"He?"

"Yes. When Seth unmade Osiris, a part of his energy was lost. His power has been diminished. He can no longer be the god he once was. If a baby is born, the piece of Osiris that Seth stole will be given to the child." Turning in his arms, Nephthys clutched his hand. "It is right and natural for parents to grant their children something of themselves."

"As the baby grows in power, he would diminish his parents," Amun-Ra protested. "They might not even survive the birth. Even with Osiris's remaining life force, there's not enough energy left to create another god. Perhaps if he was mortal . . ." His voice trailed off.

"Two gods cannot conceive a mortal child. Besides, Isis and Osiris will survive if you grant the boy a small piece of yourself as well."

Amun-Ra rubbed his jaw.

"The baby will serve as a distraction for Seth," Nephthys added. "He will waste countless decades in the pursuit of regaining the energy he will lose. He'll try every means at his disposal to unmake Isis and Osiris's child, but with the strength you lend him, Seth will remain unsuccessful."

"Nephthys, are you certain about this?" Amun-Ra asked, his eyes flickering with an unvoiced emotion. She knew he was asking about more than Isis's future son.

She beamed. "With your help, I can handle this."

"I still don't understand why marrying him was necessary. You don't love him," he stated, and yet she heard the hesitancy in his words, the underlying question.

"No. I don't. But it was a means to an end."

"Then promise me that the end, once it comes, will bring you happiness."

Taking his hand, she lifted it to her cheek and pressed a soft kiss on his palm. "I promise."

Gently, he stroked her bottom lip with his thumb. She shut her eyes, relishing the tender caress, and then he eased back and helped her stand. "I'll need to take care of this as soon as possible, then. Will you come with me?" he asked. "That is . . . if you're not in pain," he added, glancing at her back where her lovely wings used to be.

"I'll get accustomed to it. Besides, it will help to have me there. Isis will need me."

"Will you still be able to transform into a kite?"

Nephthys shook her head sadly. "The benu bird will have to fly on his own."

Amun-Ra's jaw tightened. "Then the benu bird will remain grounded until such time as you can join him again."

"That might be a very long time. Won't you miss

flying?" she asked.

He turned to her, and his eyes were full of regret and the tender new beginnings of something else. "I would miss having you by my side more," he said.

Her mouth turned up into a soft smile. "We must go," she said.

Amun-Ra took her hand and led her to his sunlit chamber, where she knew Isis and Osiris waited. With the wave of a hand he sent a summons for Seth, one that brooked no argument.

Nephthys knew that the longer she could delay her new husband from seeking his path of destruction, the better. The stars whispered to her that Wasret would not be born until the dawn of the last great age and that only she would have the power to unmake the unmaker. Until then, Nephthys must perform a complicated dance, move the pieces on the board, and keep Seth too busy to notice the mortal queen until she was ready to rise.

EPILOGUE

YIELD

Nephthys emerged from her place behind Amun-Ra's throne the moment Seth entered the room and positioned herself alongside her husband, faking a smile as she did so. Isis gave a soft gasp, which probably meant she'd noticed Nephthys's lack of wings. The act of seeing his chastised wife seemed to appease Seth, and he took hold of her hand, squeezing it possessively. Nephthys noticed Amun-Ra's frown as he glanced at their hands, and when she gave a slight shake of her head, Amun-Ra focused his frown on Isis and Osiris instead.

"Tell me everything," Amun-Ra commanded.

And they did. Isis and Osiris talked about all they'd seen Seth do, regaled Amun-Ra with information, including the fact that Seth had recently unmade the great forest, turning it into a desert so vast that even Nut could not send rain upon it. During the interview, whenever Seth tried to say something, Amun-Ra simply gave him a look and it served to stifle Seth's tongue, though he took out his anger on his wife's hand.

Despite her determination not to do so, Nephthys winced and Amun-Ra immediately noticed. "Seth," he said with an air of menace. "You will step away from your wife."

Seth obeyed, though he merely slumped into a chair with a disrespectful scowl.

"Did you use your power to kill Osiris and unmake Nephthys's wings?" Amun-Ra asked him with an expression that could freeze an erupting volcano. "Did you do all the things they accuse you of?" He indicated Isis and Osiris.

"I did," Seth answered straightforwardly. "It was . . . an accident. I didn't mean to do it. It's just that when I get angry I can't always control what I do. Besides, my new wife did the unthinkable. Nephthys diminished the

Waters of Chaos to bring back Osiris. It's unfortunate, but isn't it right that she should sacrifice something of hers to make up for it? Perhaps it was the cosmos's way of bringing back balance."

Amun-Ra ground his teeth. "You assume much, Seth. You should have brought the matter to me instead of handling it yourself."

"Isn't it a man's right to handle his own wife?" Seth asked.

Amun-Ra scoffed. "Any man, mortal or god, knows there is no handling a wife. Women handle themselves and intelligent men get out of the way. But I wouldn't expect a boy like you to know that yet."

Anger lit Seth's features, but before he could respond, Amun-Ra asked, "Speaking of being wet behind the ears, why didn't you tell the Ennead about your newly developed power?"

Seth shrugged. "I didn't want to say anything until I'd practiced more."

"I'd say you've had enough practice."

Seth's glower transformed into a crocodile smile when Amun-Ra turned his ire on Isis and Osiris. "As for you two, I'm sorry, but what you've done comes with grave consequences."

"What?" Osiris wrapped his arm around Isis, tucking her against his body. "What do you mean?"

"I mean," Amun-Ra said with a sigh, "your power, Osiris, has been diminished. You have returned to us as half the god you once were. Isis broke the rules. Not once but twice. She wove spells that reworked the nature of the cosmos. I have determined that the two of you cause trouble when you're together."

"What are you saying?" Isis demanded.

"I'm saying that there is a terrible price that must be paid. Unfortunately, the two of you will need to be separated. Osiris, you are hereby banished to the afterlife, where you will have no contact with Isis until such time as I deem the both of you have learned your lesson."

Angry tears sprang to Isis's eyes. "It wasn't his fault. It was mine! I'm the one who brought him back. Punish me."

"The afterlife is not a punishment. It is a duty," Amun-Ra said kindly. "One that Osiris will be able to manage as long as he has the help of Anubis and Ma'at. Watching over the fields there will give him a measure of peace, since he's no longer able to perform the same duties in the mortal realm."

"And what about Seth?" Isis demanded. "What is his punishment?"

Seth stifled the glee he felt over Amun-Ra's decision and attempted to adopt a mien of contriteness.

"Seth will make a vow not to use his power against any of the gods ever again. He will be closely supervised by me. I promise you."

"That's all?" Osiris asked. "After everything he's done, he just gets a rebuke best reserved for a naughty child?"

"You are not to question my decisions," Amun-Ra said. "Your job is to see to your duties." He leaned forward, an expression of sympathy on his face as he turned to the weeping goddess. "I am sorry for this. I truly am. But know this is for your own good. I will grant the two of you a reprieve until tomorrow. Take comfort in the love you feel for one another tonight and I'll send Anubis to fetch Osiris in the morning.

"As for you." He turned to Seth. "Until you have demonstrated to me sufficiently that you know how to treat a wife, you will keep your hands off this one."

The corner of Seth's mouth turned down and he

lowered his head in a mock bow. "As you wish," he replied faintly.

"And you will not bother these two this night. Let them say goodbye. They will remain in Heliopolis, where they will spend their remaining hours together, and you will spend the evening on Earth and consider the things you have wrought." Amun-Ra narrowed his gaze on Seth. "I will know if you breach the boundary between our realms."

"Of course, mighty one," Seth said. He gave Nephthys a thoughtful glance, but she shook her head, indicating she was not going to accompany him. Truthfully, he preferred to be on his own for the time being anyway. Tucking his hands behind his back, he made his way to the barrier separating the realms.

As he disappeared through with a pop, he smiled. Let them have their one night together. He'd have the next day and the day after. Isis would forget Osiris before the year was out. After that it would be only a matter of time until he could sway Isis to his side. With her ability to create spells, he could have anything he wanted. He could even depose Amun-Ra himself. Rubbing his hands as he emerged from the barrier, he lifted his nose to the wind and wondered what fearsome creature he could next unmake.

* * *

An hour later, Nephthys knocked on Amun-Ra's door.

"Come in," he called.

When he saw it was her, he rose and took her hand, settling her into the soft chair next to his, the ones where they often took tea together. "How is she?" he asked.

"As can be expected. Osiris has whisked her away."

"Did you tell her about Cherty?"

Nephthys nodded. "I gave her a bag full of your stamped coins. Then I told her Cherty could be bribed to take her to see her husband and that as long as she took care of her responsibilities, no one would be the wiser."

"Good," he said.

"She asked about the true names. She wants me to tell her Seth's."

"What did you say?"

"I said that only you had access to that."

"That's smart. It means she'll come after me. She doesn't need to know that even I don't know his true name."

"She thinks I love him," Nephthys said.

"Did you tell her the truth?"

"I merely replied, 'It's better to have loved and lost than never to have loved at all.'"

Amun-Ra picked up her hand and traced his fingertips across the back of it. "Do you believe that?" he asked, feeling as if everything in him hung upon her answer.

Nephthys eyes gleamed as they looked at each other. "No," she answered simply. "Love, once found, is never lost."

KEEP READING FOR BONUS

CHAPTER OF THE NEXT BOOK

IN THE REAWAKENED SERIES

Reunited

BY COLLEEN HOUCK

The Snare Of Love

With snare in hand I hide me,
I wait and will not stir;
The beauteous birds of Araby
Are perfumed all with myrrh
Oh all the birds of Araby,
That down to Egypt come,
Have wings that waft the fragrance
Of sweetly smelling gum!
I would that, when I snare them,
Together we could be,
I would that when I hear them
Alone I were with thee.
If thou wilt come, my dear one,
When birds are snared above,
I'll take thee and I'll keep thee
Within the snare of love.

***From Egyptian Myths And Legend**

By Donald Mackenzie

Prologue

Entombed

"It begins."

"Yes, Master. The chains that bind you are weakening."

"It was foolish of them to think that this prison would hold me indefinitely."

The darkness that surrounded Seth sat upon his shoulders like a burial shroud weighted with lead. What remained of his grandmother, Tefnut, who once controlled the waters of the earth and sky, swirled around his form—trapping, immobilizing, suffocating.

When he'd first been imprisoned, Tefnut's etheric

waters lapped against his consciousness and dragged him down to the depths of the blackest holes in the universe, where he was swallowed up. Seth couldn't imagine any kind of punishment that would have been worse. Admittedly, he'd caused the painful deaths of countless beings, but their lives were insignificant. They were flies. No. They were the tiny microscopic organisms that lived on the backs of flies.

And, yes, he'd unmade the golden, all-too-perfect Osiris. But Isis had brought him back, hadn't she?

Isis.

Just thinking about her made his blood boil.

And Nephthys? His estranged wife who had supported the gods when they'd decided to trap him in the obelisk of eternity?

His fingers itched to wrap around her throat. Thinking of the two goddesses and what he'd do to them once he was free was the only thing that brought him pleasure in his black dungeon. Even Nut, his own mother, had abandoned him.

As he hung suspended beneath Tefnut's dark waves, he almost forgot who he was.

What he was.

Almost.

Still, it might have been a peaceful incarceration if it hadn't been for Shu. The god of the wind had decided he no longer wanted to exist without his wife, Tefnut, so Shu caught hold of her life force as it lifted away. Speeding through the cosmos, he joined his soul with hers in a sleep of death, fully knowing there'd be no turning back. Together they ensnared him in a net so powerful, there was no escape. Or so they believed.

What a waste of godly powers.

Seth had puzzled over the years why his grandparents had done it.

Oh, he knew *why* they'd done it.

His immortal family all believed that nothing short of a god's sacrifice would be able to hold him. In that they were right.

The part that Seth didn't understand was why Shu couldn't live without his wife.

Tefnut was a cranky old bat. Her moods were as changeable as the weather. Of course, Shu was a hot bag of wind himself—constantly preaching to anyone who would listen about right and wrong. And Shu definitely believed there were all kinds of wrong that needed to be fixed where Seth was concerned.

Still, to give up. To relinquish all that Shu was. For

a woman. The concept baffled him.

As he considered the idea, the wind that comprised the remains of what was once his grandfather Shu, buffeted against him and then all too quickly, faded away—a pathetic showing when compared to what had trapped him for so long. Its force had screamed in his mind for millennia—hurtling a cyclone of accusations and censure. Now the winds were so weak, he could no longer hear Shu's voice in the gale.

Seth was almost sad that what they'd once been, two of the most powerful gods in the cosmos, had diminished to the point of disappearing. They'd willingly sacrificed their immortality just because Amun-Ra convinced them that his plan for the cosmos was right and Seth's was wrong.

Shu and Tefnut had been his only companions over the centuries. He knew what remained of them was not truly them. The wind and the waves were simply echoes of what they once were—fingerprints left behind. He siphoned off as much of their energy as he was able before their power waned and returned to the Waters of Chaos. Still, it wasn't enough. His prison limited his abilities. Drained him dry.

That he'd allowed the gods to trick him into his prison at

all galled him hour after gloomy hour. At least he'd been wise enough to keep the feather of Isis on his person at all times. It had gone undiscovered and the healing properties it gifted him, helped sustain him. Kept him sane. Well at least as sane as one could be when trapped in an oubliette for centuries. Luckily it wasn't a normal feather. Otherwise his continual stroking of its downy edges would have worn it all the way to the shaft within a week.

Seth despaired of ever escaping, of ever seeing the light of day again.

But then, he felt the walls that trapped him weaken. It took eons to wear down the barrier separating him from his traitorous family. He pushed against the confines of his prison, feeling for any spark he could draw from in the outside world.

Then, a spark found him. A human, an ordinary sort of man, discovered a scroll, long forgotten, that held a spell powerful enough to draw a thread from the dark tapestry that fell like a curtain over his mind. The man must have been touched by magic. Perhaps he was the descendant of an immortal.

For a time, he wondered who had left the spell, and why. Could there be an ally living among those that hated him? The thought that it might be Isis skittered through his mind. Had she finally seen through the all-too-winsome smile of her husband? Did she regret banishing Seth? Trapping him in the obelisk? He longed to know and spent countless hours pondering the implications. Eventually, Seth decided that he didn't care how it happened, just that it did.

The mortal used the spell.

It was a tiny change. A chip in a wall of cement. Minuscule when you considered the power channeled into maintaining his prison. But it was enough. Seth took hold of the thread very carefully and pulled. As he did, his mind's eye connected to that of the mortal. It wasn't instantaneous, but in the course of a few years, what surmounted to the blink of an eye to Seth, he'd been able to siphon energy from others and imbue the immortal with power. Enough power that he would have a chance to stop the Sons of Egypt from reinforcing his prison.

Unfortunately, it didn't work. The mortal proved too weak to accomplish his goal. But just before his minion was killed, Seth stole back the mortal's energy and unmade his creation. Power filled him and he pressed against the barrier with all of his might.

Reignited Discussion Guide

1. Seth felt unloved, unappreciated, and untalented when compared with his siblings. Is he entirely to blame for the person he became and the choices he made?

2. Seth's power is perhaps the greatest of all second only to Amun-Ra. Compare and contrast their abilities. How are they two sides of the same coin?

3. Isis tells her sister, Nephthys, the secret wishes of her heart. What are Nephthys' secret wishes?

4. Isis knows of the edict forbidding love between the gods and yet she still falls for Osiris, is forbidden love sweeter or more desirable?

5. What is Isis willing to sacrifice for Baniti? What is their relationship?

6. Nephthys knows more about what's going on

than she shares. Why do you think she keeps information from Isis?

7. Would you rather have the power to unmake or to create? Why?

8. The adder stone is a symbol in the series. Lily is often referred to as an adder stone and in REIGNITED there is an actual adder stone on top of a mountain. What is the purpose of such a place and why do you think it is important in the story?

9. All the characters in this book are called upon to make sacrifices. What are they and does Seth sacrifice anything?

10. Many of the gods and goddesses, despite their great power, feel lonely. Why? How is Seth's destruction of an ecosystem a symbol of this?

11. Does Seth really love Isis or does he just want to absorb her power into himself? How do you know?

12. How would the story have changed if Isis and Osiris had not fallen in love? Would Seth have pursued the same path?

13. Osiris does not see the danger in Seth as easily as Isis. Is he blind to it or does he still dismiss him as being less than?

14. If Nephthys knew what kind of a husband Seth would be, why did she marry him?

15. How does knowing the origin story of the gods and goddesses influence your understanding of Lily's story?

16. Was the bond created between Isis and Osiris the same as Lily's and Amon's?

17. How is the goddess Isis different in REIGNITED than in RECREATED? How does losing your love affect you?

18. What is Seth really trying to accomplish in this book? Are his goals attainable?

19. Which character grew the most in the course of this book? Why do you think so?

20. How has your understanding of Egyptian mythology changed by reading this story? Does it fit with what you know of the traditional tales?

Acknowledgements

I think I've been lax in thanking my dogs. I was out with a group of writers recently and we were talking about having little pet companions and which types were the best for writers. Writing is a lonely job and having a faithful companion at your feet or to snuggle during times when you get stuck is very helpful, so thank you to Bitsy and Murphy and to my late little poodle Prissy for being my constant sidekicks.

I'd also like to thank my agent, Robert Gottleib, for his staunch support in my behalf. He always has my back and has been extremely generous with his time and attention.

Reignited is a passion project and I am grateful for the chance to develop the story and the character of my villain. I've always believed a hero is only as strong as the villain he or she fights.

I have several nieces and nephews who sneak peeks over their mom's shoulders to see what I'm writing next and to always wants arcs to show off at school the minute they show up at my door. Their enthusiasm keeps me going and even the boys are proud enough to wear their promotional tees at book events and help me run my PowerPoints.

Deep appreciation goes to my editor, Krista Vitola, to the Delacorte team including Krista Vitola and Colleen Fellingham, and to the team at Trident Media Group, including Alicia Granstein, Nicole Robson, Emily Ross and Brianna Weber. Your dedication to your craft means the world to me.

Lastly, I'd like to thank my readers. You guys are all awesome and I wish we could plan a trip to Egypt and India together. =)

ABOUT THE AUTHOR

Colleen Houck is the *New York Times* bestselling author of the Tiger's Curse series and the Reawakened series. Her books have appeared on the *USA Today*, *Publishers Weekly*, and Walmart bestseller lists, among many others. She has been a Parents' Choice Award winner and has been reviewed and featured on MTV.com and in the *Los Angeles Times*, *USA Today*, *Girls' Life* magazine, and *Romantic Times*, which called *Tiger's Curse* "one of the best books I have ever read." Colleen lives in Salem, Oregon, with her husband and a huge assortment of plush tigers.